OTHER BOOKS BY BILL GOURGEY

Attic Ward (Cap City Mysteries, Book 2)
Court Kasie (Cap City Mysteries, Book 3)
Castle Keep (Cap City Mysteries, Book 4)
Gravity & Fire (Glide Trilogy, Book 1)
Games & Fate (Glide Trilogy, Book 2)
Germs & Fury (Glide Trilogy, Book 3)
Unfamiliar Fruit, *Short Stories*
Outside the Box, *Poems*

The Beverly Hills Book Award–winning author of the Glide Trilogy delivers an emotionally charged story of hard luck and hope in the nation's capital.

When thirteen-year-old Boot doesn't have the money to pay his mom's drug dealer, he must flee or face certain death at the hands of the gang leader who rules his DC neighborhood. The glittering dome of the United States Capitol Building, which looks like the Emerald City of Oz from across the Anacostia River, seems like an ideal hide out until Boot discovers that the halls of Congress may not be all that different from the ruthless streets he fled. In Capitol Kid, a well-heeled politician at the pinnacle of power squares off with a savvy street urchin in a thrilling showdown that shakes Washington, DC.

A Rare View of the Gilded Halls of Congress
From the Senate Chamber's renowned Candy Desk to bizarre accounts of murder and intrigue in the halls of Congress, this book is peppered with eye-popping historical facts of one of our nation's most prominent landmarks: the U.S. Capitol Building.

You Won't Look At Your Smartphone the Same Way Ever Again
Is it really true that your phone's camera and mic can be hacked? Ever wonder if your IDs and passwords are safe? This book offers a chilling account of how readily available apps and black-market devices can be used to spy on our every conversation and keystroke. It's fiction, but just barely

This fast-paced book will make you laugh, cry, and will keep you on the edge of your seat!

Praise for *Cap City Mysteries*

"Gourgey's smart mystery-thriller is a well-constructed game of wits."
—BookLife Prize for Fiction Critic's Report (*Capitol Kid*)

"Gourgey masterfully conveys not only the angst of being a teenager but also the courage and resourcefulness that a talented, impassioned young person can muster."
—Literary Hill (*Attic Ward*)

"A page turner. I'd love to see this as a movie."
—Amazon reviewer (*Capitol Kid*)

Praise for Bill Gourgey's Other Stories

"Gourgey conjures up dazzlingly innovative concepts that wickedly satirize online interactions and offer mind-spinning visions of futuristic technologies."
—*Publishers Weekly Select* (*Glide Trilogy*, 2015)

"I loved this book! I found myself thinking about the characters well after I finished reading."
—Amazon reviewer (*Unfamiliar Fruit*, 2013)

"Gourgey employs tension extraordinarily well, ratcheting up the suspense from beginning to end, so that when the final confrontation takes place, it is a cathartic explosion of pent-up nerves."
—Aaron Pound, *Dreaming About Other Worlds* (*Glide Trilogy*, 2013)

CAPITOL KID

BY

BILL GOURGEY

Jacked Arts
Washington, DC 20008
www.jackedarts.com

Library of Congress Control Number: 2015913919

Print ISBN: 978-0-9894205-7-0
eBook ISBN: 978-0-9894205-8-7

Front Cover Font: Montserrat.
Front Cover Photo: Man running out of tunnel by AMR, iStockPhoto.

Title Page interior graphic by Yevhen Verlen (Abstract Background) and Fernando Jose Vascocelos Soares (Two people silhouette), dreamstime.com.

Title Page Font: 1968 GLC Graffiti (Open Type) by Gilles Le Corre.

For Sawyer

and for Jen, Art, and their Parks Clan

CONTENTS

CAPITOL KID

HOME SUITE HOME

*H*ey you, kid!" I hear Rhino holler. He's angry, as usual, and he has his hand clasped to the butt of his gun, as if he'd really pull it from its holster and shoot me.

Not in here, he wouldn't.

This is the sacred Senate Chamber of the United States Capitol Building, engine of the world's greatest democracy, where the laws of this great land get debated in earnest, and the plight of the people is always foremost—

"I've got you now, kid!" Rhino growls. His knees are bent and he's leaning slightly forward to catch his breath. One hand's on his holster and the other's hitched to the side of his belt, which looks like a portable hardware store. Besides his gun, there are extra rounds, a flashlight, walkie-talkie, can of mace, water bottle, billy club, badge, Leatherman knife, and a few other doodads. Even without all that gear, he'd be lumbering around. He's carrying an extra seventy-five pounds (at least) that he can't blame on his uniform.

Rhino undoes the snap on his holster, but leaves the gun in its place. That's one of my advantages: I know it would take a lot for him to pull a gun in this sanctuary. But guns weren't always taboo.

Back in the good old days when "*remote*" meant the Oregon Trail, not an electronics accessory, senators used to carry their own guns—and knives, and canes—right onto the Senate floor. Well, technically, that was in the Old Senate Chamber. But imagine if they were allowed to carry guns today? The way these politicians hate each other, it would be like *Saints Row* meets *Call of Duty*. I mean, the amount of ammunition unloaded in here would be like when Neo and Trinity took on the Matrix agents to save Morpheus. It would make the O.K. Corral look like a chit chat.

I should know; I see these politicians every day (that is, when they're working), even if they don't see me.

Rhino's standing in the well of the Chamber, and I'm several rows up, so he can't see anything below my waist, which is good because I've just finished dumping my bag full of dead cockroaches (the ones I collected from the kitchen) into the Candy Desk—desk #24. Back in 1965, Senator Charles Murphy started the tradition of keeping sweets in his desk, and ever since then there's been this Candy Desk. I forget who sits here now, although the senator's name is probably carved in the drawer. Name carving is one of the Senate traditions. Try to get away with *that* in school.

But I don't have time to check whose desk this is. I don't want Rhino to catch on to what I'm doing or he'll clear out the roaches before the senators get to sample them.

I'm deft with my hands—learned to master the five-finger discount before I was nine—so I ease the drawer shut, tuck some real candy into my waistband, lift my hands in the air, palms out, shoulder high to show I'm clean, and back slowly up the aisle.

There's no way Rhino will catch me before I split through the nearest door at the top of the Chamber. There's lots of ways in and out of this place.

"In your dreams, old man!" I taunt Rhino. He hates being called old man. Technically, he's not old, but he's a lot older than me, and he's fat and bald and has a long, pointy nose and eyes that are too small for his round head, which is why I call him Rhino.

A wicked grin spreads across Rhino's face, which sends a chill up my spine. He's got something up his sleeve. Suddenly, his guards file in through the two doors behind me and the one to my right. I calculate my odds. Even though I'm only thirteen (almost fourteen), and every one of these guys is twice my weight (except Chase), way stronger than me (including Chase), and fully armed, I'm no shrimp for my age. I'm lean, and I have lots of practice escaping the law. Plus, when you're the prey and you're hemmed in like this, you have two advantages: 1) your predators are inevitably overconfident, licking their chops too soon; and 2) the cornered prey effect kicks in. It's well known that cornered prey put up ferocious fights that often astonish their opponents. It's called adrenaline. And I feel mine pumping now.

"Hey Melon," I say to the tallest guard who's closing in fast. His bulging arm muscles, amplified by black arm bands, look like he's hiding melons inside them. "Better duck or I'll dissolve you with my fireballs." With that, I reach into my waistband and hurl the candy I nabbed from the Candy Desk. I wouldn't try that *Super Mario Brothers* trick out on the streets or I'd be eating bullets, but Melon is so stupid that he predictably hits the deck like I launched real fireballs at him.

I laugh and take off toward the far end of the Chamber where two doors remain unguarded.

That's a third advantage. If you get your opponents fired up enough, they'll lose their cool and won't think. Losing your cool is more common in this Chamber than you would guess. Like, this is where Representative Preston Brooks caned Senator Charles Sumner nearly to death for calling his cousin out as a friend to slavery in his infamous Crime Against Kansas speech in 1856. It's where Senator Ben Tillman punched Senator John McLaurin in the mouth for lying about his character (1902). And where Senator Strom Thurmond filibustered for more than twenty-four hours against the Civil Rights Act in 1957. I could go on about the ill tempers and bizarre beliefs of senators and congressmen, but I don't have time right now.

Melon's back on his feet and slavering like he's rabid. He lunges at me, but even he can't clear the two rows he needs to catch up. I hear him crash into a couple of desks behind me. I'll give him credit—he nearly nipped my heels. Now that I'm past Melon, it's a footrace to the other side.

Chase, the only female guard on Rhino's *elite* team, has no chance of catching me, but she's dodging through the desks anyway. I kind of like Chase. I don't know if it's her gray eyes and mane of chestnut hair, or the she-warrior look that remind me of Annabeth Chase, brainchild of Athena in *Percy Jackson* (great books, good movies, lousy video games), but she seems smarter than the rest of Rhino's crew. Plus, she's fast. She's the only one I worry about catching me in a footrace. I hear a loud thud and groan as Chase's thigh catches one of the desks wrong and she falls sideways.

Rhino knows he's going to lose. Again. "Stop or I'll shoot!" he hollers. I turn to look at him. He actually has his gun trained on me. Now *that's* a surprise. But I know he'd catch hell if he pulled the trigger in here.

"No, you won't," I call over my shoulder. Then I slip through the doors and slam them shut on Loki (who has jet-black hair and a naturally devious expression) just as he's about to come through. Loki had been sneaking down the side of the Senate Chamber like he was wearing an invisibility cloak or something. But I spotted him right from the beginning. I hear a grunt followed by a loud thud and know that I knocked Loki off his feet.

Time to get lost.

That's what I love about the Capitol Building: it's an endless maze. In fact, it's more like a luxury hotel than a government building, with its secret halls, underground passageways, domes, rotundas, galleys, corridors, peristyles, offices, committee rooms, balconies, dining rooms, elevators, garages, libraries, a crypt (well, maybe that isn't a luxury hotel feature unless it's serving vampires), and even a private underground train! Most people don't know the half of it, and not even the people who work here know about the secret passages and rooms built beneath the Capitol that spread out into the surrounding nabes like a giant underground web. I bet not even the Architect of the Capitol Building—the Architect is like the Pope of this place, overseeing all maintenance activity on the grounds, new construction, that sort of thing (there have been only eleven Architects since 1793; talk about job security!)—I bet not even the Architect knows about some of these secret passages. That's how I found my hideout (I'll tell you about it later), and that's where I've been living.

But now, I feel like finding my favorite spot, which is on the roof. I can only go there when Congress is not in session. Otherwise, there's Capitol Police up there and sometimes Secret Service—except when the weather's nasty (as if terrorists and bad guys don't go out on rainy days). Maybe water makes these *elite* law enforcement agents melt like wicked witches.

I sprint down the richly decorated hall (parts of this place are like a palace), my high tops slapping the shiny marble, and plunge into a service stairwell. Two flights up, I stop to listen. Nothing. As expected. I've ditched the guards again.

One of these days, Rhino really will shoot, but until then, I'm gonna keep calling this place home. I climb to the top of the stairs and push open the metal door to the roof. It's heavy, and slams shut with a loud clang. But it's pretty late—after midnight—so nobody will hear it.

As soon as I'm standing on the roof, I feel a stiff breeze blowing off the river. The fresh air feels good. It's crisp, November air. A little chilly for these rags I'm wearing, but I have a cozy little nest to snuggle into later. I rub the backs of my arms and, knowing exactly where the security cameras are positioned, weave my way to the edge of the roof, somewhere above the Majority Leader of the Senate's luxurious balcony. I sit there, on the edge, swinging my legs, and look out over the Mall.

Off to my right is Union Station where trains come and go, day and night. It might be my imagination, but I think I hear an air horn now, signaling that a train's on the move—that's such a hopeful sound. Straight ahead, the Washington Monument is lit up like a giant candle. Ant-Man, my best friend in Southeast (or anywhere), calls it the nation's junk, and I know he's only partly talking about trash. But I like the Monument, and Lincoln's Memorial beyond, which is lit up, too, like a pharaoh's tomb. Don't get me wrong. I'm not stupid. I know the politicians in this part of town don't care about people like me—we're like cockroaches to them—but I still love this view and what it represents. Freedom. I don't have freedom, not like it was meant to be, but I like the idea of it. My mom, when she was sober, always did say I was a romantic. Not exactly sure what she meant, since I've never had a girlfriend, but I think she was referring to my starry-eyed outlook on life.

My real name is Boot. Well, that's not my *real* name, but it's what everyone's called me for as long as I can remember. At first they used to call me that because I'd always be getting the "boot in the booty" from my parents, who never liked having me around when it was adult time (especially my dad), which was just another excuse for having parties and getting so high they couldn't talk. So I'd have to sleep in the hall of our tenement, or under the overpass if the nights were too hot and the smell in the hall too bad. Sometimes, Ant-Man would let me crash at his place, or our neighbor Mrs. Smith would take me in, but that gets old real fast. People are willing to help each other out as long as it's not indefinite. Everyone always knew my situation was definitely indefinite.

When I got a little older, everyone kept on calling me Boot because I was good with computers. I'm good at school, too, although I pretty much stopped going. It's boring and dangerous, and I like to avoid risk of injury. It's a good mantra to live by.

My guidance counselor had me take a test last year. She was surprised when I scored off the charts on everything. When I made a wise crack about it, she added that I was too smart for my own good, and that it would get me in serious trouble someday. But she also said I had the highest IQ of anyone she's ever known. I felt like saying, *like a high IQ does me any good around here.* I'd rather be strong and stupid. A lion wearing glasses doesn't get to dine with the other lions. I don't really wear glasses, but people think I'm a geek. I mean, I can recall just about anything I've ever seen or heard—but a good memory doesn't deflect bullets or pay off your mom's drug dealer.

My computer skills started with fixing video game systems—PlayStations, Xboxes, Wiis, Game Boys, even an Atari Jaguar once, which had to be from the 1990s. You name it, and I could fix it.

I got a part-time job when I was eight (off the books), working at LaQuota's pawnshop, Come Up. By the way, she spells it *L"a.* Believe it or not, that's her name. Says she's got some Cajun blood so she wanted something that sounded French. She changed her name a long time ago, but I don't know what her real name is. Since she's a leader, not a follower, she invented her own name, something with more than one ironic twist to it.

LaQuota took pity on me after my dad left, and started letting me hang around her shop. When she figured out I had a knack for electronics, she put me to work. Now, whenever someone brings in stolen laptops, tablets, or smartphones, I hack into them, scrub the passwords and all the other identifying data, reboot them, load them up with pirated software that I set up on a server in the backroom of LaQuota's shop, and she sells them for a sweet profit.

Come Up is on the second floor of the row house LaQuota owns (she told me it's called a double entendre when something has two meanings, like her store's name). The first floor is a bodega, and LaQuota lives on the third floor with her lover, Dottie. (Yeah, you guessed it, spelled *.e.* But Dottie only started spelling it that way when she moved in with LaQuota.) LaQuota and Dottie are lesbians, which some people think is messed up, but I don't. They're good to me. Plus, they have just about the most stable relationship of anyone I know.

My real name is Henry. Henry Thomas, Jr.

Henry Thomas, Sr., my dad, is locked up for life on account of first-degree manslaughter. It wasn't his first offense.

My mom (her name's Juanita) is probably in some crack house or bar somewhere across the river. I miss her, but I haven't talked to her since I moved in here a couple of months ago. She'd like my new digs. She'd like it all lit up at night like this. She's from Miami. Said she always liked night better because it was cooler.

I pull my phone from my pocket. One of the perks

working for LaQuota is that she lets me have my own gear. So I have a laptop, two smartphones, and a smartwatch (which is lame). She won't let me have a tablet because they fetch top dollar and sell like hotcakes, but that's OK—I already snatched one from some Senate staffers. Nabbed a few smartphones, too. It's always good to have some extra parts lying around. Plus, I hack their phones for passwords and contact data. It's amazing to me how much stuff people leave on their phones. People don't realize it, but phones are easy to hack. Storing personal data on them is like walking down the street with your wallet hanging out, wearing a placard that says Mug Me.

I use the passwords to access some of the different Wi-Fi networks around here, so I can get online. That's how I know all that stuff about the history of this place. Been reading up at night. I'm not much of a movie or TV show watcher. I'd rather play a video game or even read a good book. My mom always did say I was too smart for my own good.

I pop in the one legit SIM card I have, and hit Ant-Man's name on my list of contacts (it's the only number I have beside my mom's and LaQuota's).

"Yo, I must be talkin' to a ghost." It's Ant-Man's raspy voice. He smokes so much he'll probably have throat cancer by the time he's twenty.

"Ha, ha," I say.

"Where ya been, bro?" Ant-Man asks. I can hear lots of voices in the background. He must have people over. His parents are never around, working all the time, but they have one of the nicest houses on the street. So Ant-Man (his real name's Antonio, but when he's wearing his gaming gear he reminds me of the Marvel Comics hero Ant-Man) takes full advantage.

"Had to disappear," I say.

"No kidding. And you better stay away, too. If Stang catches up with you, he's gonna slice off your balls and stuff 'em down your throat. Just like he did to The Wizard. What did you do to Stang anyway?"

"It's complicated," I say. My shoulders slump. I was hoping that things would cool off if I lay low for a while. But Stang holds grudges. The Wizard that Ant-Man mentioned was a two-bit dealer that Stang used to supply. *Used to.* The Wizard disappeared last year. They found his body in the Anacostia River. Everyone knows Stang killed him.

Stang gets his nickname from his Mustang cars. That's *cars* with an *s*. He has a bunch of Mustangs, all of them tricked out. I hear he even races some of them at a track somewhere in Virginia.

"Everything's complicated," Ant-Man says, laughing. I can hear him lighting up. "You want me to talk to him?" he offers, holding his breath.

"Na. You don't want to get involved."

"I was joking, bro. But I miss you. There are no strait-laced geeks around here to make fun of!" He starts laughing again. "Hey, check out these pics."

Suddenly, a handful of Snapchats come in with selfies of Ant-Man and some of the girls from the nabe draping their arms around him like he was the big man on campus.

I grin. "Call me if anything changes," I say. I hesitate because I know he won't be able to call me since I only pop in my real SIM card every few days to see if my mom or LaQuota tried to reach me. I'm afraid to use my real SIM since I know they can be used for tracking. But Ant-Man won't call me. Not unless the world is crashing and burning. "See ya, bro," I say, and end the call.

I swear under my breath. *This is your fault, Mom.*

Ever since I was eight, my mom used me as her drug runner. As if I was some drugstore delivery boy. Only, the drugstore was Stang's place, and the drugs were illegal. Mostly heroin. By the time I was nine, I caught on. By the time I was twelve, I resented it. I resented her, and Stang, and his Atlantic Terrace crew, and just about everyone in my nabe for tolerating all the drugs. Sometimes I even resent Ant-Man even though he's my friend. It's why I hate drugs.

Then, a couple of months ago, when I went to make a pickup for my mom, Stang started to beat me because I didn't have any money to give him. I snapped. It was just me and him in his apartment. Luckily, his dogs—two giant charcoal-and-white pit bulls—were locked up. When he started punching and kicking me, I grabbed a baseball bat that was lying on the couch (he was known to use it from time to time on other cowering customers) and began fighting back. I beat him pretty good. Knocked him unconscious. When I realized what I'd done, I disappeared. It was sheer luck that I found a secret entrance to the Capitol Building. Been living here since.

I know my mom needs me. I've called her a couple of times, but I hang up whenever she answers. She's tried texting me, but I don't reply. She does whatever Stang tells her. I know she loves me, but she'd set me up in a heartbeat if it meant getting a small bag to smoke.

A strong gust blows off the river. This one has hints of

winter in it. I shiver and rub the backs of my arms. Then I take one last look across the sparkling city and retreat down the stairs. As I said, there's a whole other complex down below the Capitol Building that most people don't know about. That's where I have my own room. It's a luxury suite compared to what I'm used to. Been collecting things to fix it up.

I call it Home Suite Home.

MS. VERITA

I can tell Congress is in session even before I open my eyes and even though I'm still in my subbasement room. Want to know my secret? The calendar alarm on my cell phone has a different ring tone—a riff from Maroon 5, "Animals." I keep track of Congress's calendar. Have to. Whenever Congress is in session, security is that much tighter, plus there are a lot more people everywhere. I have to be extra careful.

I kick off the blankets I've gathered from various staff rooms (I even lifted a famous quilt from the senator of Wyoming's office) and roll out of the cot, which to me is the most luxurious mattress I've ever slept on. I yawn, stretch, and flick on my laptop. While it's resuming, I grab a power bar and apple from my large stash (the bananas are too bruised), and settle into the leather office chair I managed to drag down here. My laptop is set up on a folding table that they use when arranging buffets for staffers who are pulling all-nighters.

When I first moved in, it didn't take me long to figure out how to hack into the Capitol complex's virtual private network (VPN) using Rhino's ID and password. Some system administrator was stupid enough to give Rhino admin access (well, I guess he *is* head of Capitol security), and Rhino is stupid enough to use his smartphone to log on to the network. I'm telling you, hacking smartphones is like two plus two. All I had to do was get Rhino's phone number—not too difficult to find in the directory—and send him an anonymous text using one of the many malware programs that anyone can download from the web. The text had a link to a jailbreak app called Pangu (it's for iPhones; if Rhino had an Android phone, I would have used Rootland). As soon as Rhino clicked the text I sent (which was an offer for free pizza from Jack's Pizza down the street) it downloaded the Pangu app onto his phone, which opened it up for me to access remotely. There are a couple of other steps, but not many. It's really that simple. Within fifteen minutes, I was able to set up my own ID. Rhino doesn't even know I still own his phone—virtually, that is.

Now, from the comfort of my underground suite, I'm able to scan just about every room in the building by tapping into the same surveillance feeds that the guards use to monitor activity in the various buildings and grounds. There are more than fifteen buildings—really big ones— that make up the Capitol complex, plus things like the Botanic Garden and Supreme Court. Whenever Congress is in session, I make a point of monitoring Representative Bridges's office. She's the House Majority Leader. When I bring up the feed, I'm not disappointed. It's not Representative Bridges I'm after, but her Legislative Director, Ms. Verita. At the moment, Ms. Verita is sitting across the desk from Representative Bridges, and is facing the security camera perfectly. I sigh. She's so beautiful.

I bring up my laptop's webcam so I can look at myself side by side with Ms. Verita.

Ugh! Just about the only thing I have going for me are my eyes, which my mother always called electrifying ("electrizante")—one's hazel, the other's brown. "Mijito, with those long lashes and caramel curls, you're going to be a woman slayer someday," my mom would say, fingering my shoulder length curls. That was when she was sober. She also called me a mutt—part white, part African, part Latino, part Asian. She told me that was why I had two different colored eyes. "¡Y mira!" she would joke in her thick accent, "you're probably even part Cherokee."

To me, my face is too thin, my teeth all crooked—one has a big chip in it—and even my mulatto skin ("café con leche," my mom calls it) looks naturally dirty. It's really hard to sneak a shower in this place. Half of my left eyebrow is missing from the time I fell off a stone wall trying to escape the cops. I run my fingers along a deep gash in my chin from Darrell (he's part of Stang's Atlantic Terrace crew), who cut me with a bottle when I was ten as payback for my mom stealing drugs from Stang. And I have a thin scar along my cheekbone in the shape of a hook—that one came from my dad's belt buckle. That scar means something to me, like a badge of honor. I got it trying to pull my dad off my mom one night. She was high and he was drunk.

With all that mileage, I guess I look older than I am. Street life will do that to a kid.

I stare at Ms. Verita. She's a Latina Marilyn Monroe—mole, pillow lips, curvy hips, sassy hair and all. Only her skin is mocha and her eyes dark chocolate. Today, she's wearing a blue dress the color of the sky. (I know, most security feeds are the fuzzy, black-and-white, convenience-store kind, but here in Congress, they can afford to store high-def video on their surveillance servers.) I sigh again. Even though Ms. Verita is more than twice my age, I actually think I'm in love with her. I look at myself again. She's a queen, and I'm just a grimy peasant. Cinderella with the roles reversed.

In disgust, I close my webcam window and begin scheming. I have to figure out how to see her today. She's one of the few staffers I've met, and the only staffer who is kind of like a friend. There's a general rumor around Congress about me, but mostly it's kept quiet because I'm an embarrassment to Rhino and his United States Capitol Police team. If any of the senators or representatives know, they don't talk about it. Officially, I can't exist, or they'd have to acknowledge there's a problem. And that's OK with me.

But Ms. Verita knows me; she's my only ally, although I'm sure she would say that's stretching it.

I first met Ms. Verita a month ago when she and her staff were pulling an all-nighter to get a bill ready for Representative Bridges. Whenever the staffers work all night like that, they set up a dinner buffet in a nearby conference room and switch it to breakfast in the mornings. I use my video surveillance access to scan the grounds and find those buffets because they can be a real gold mine. Usually, if I wait until two or three in the morning, I can have my pick of what's left—and they always order way too much—before the maintenance crew comes to clean it all up. On this particular night, I was filling my makeshift backpack when Ms. Verita walked into the room. I'd never seen her before.

"Hey, kid, what do you think you're doing?" she said. I could tell by the look on her face that she was more surprised than scared or angry.

"Figured no one else was gonna eat it," I said, shrugging and moving to put the buffet table between us.

"Who are you?"

I learned early on that the best lies always have a kernel of truth. "They call me 'Kid,'" I said, shouldering my bag and grabbing a biscuit. I figured I could launch it at her if I needed a distraction to scoot by her and out the door.

She planted her fists on her hips. "Who are *they*?"

"The guards."

"I'm calling security," she said, whipping out her phone.

"I wouldn't do that." I shrugged and edged my way to the end of the table until I had a straight path to the door—not counting Ms. Verita, who was standing in the way.

"Give me one good reason why I shouldn't?" Ms. Verita asked, holding her phone in her palm, her finger perched above the keypad.

"I'll give you two." I held up two fingers. "First, Rhino and his crew are imbeciles. Y además, soy muy inteligente. Y esto podría ser muy útil." I tapped the side of my head with my finger.

I could tell Ms. Verita approved of my use of Spanish. *Thanks, Mom.* I could also see that she was trying to work out whether or not my claim was true about being useful. "¿Quién es Rhino?"

"El capitán. The captain of the guards."

Ms. Verita laughed at that. "You mean Lonnigan? I guess he does look like a rhinoceros." She laughed some more and put her phone away.

That's when I knew Ms. Verita was on my side. She invited me to sit and eat with her. I shared as little as I could about myself. She was guarded, too. But I did tell her that I had checked into Hotel Capitol for a short stay. At first she thought it was funny. When she realized I wasn't kidding, she told me it was really stupid, that it was a huge breach of national security in addition to the usual petit crimes of trespassing and breaking and entering. (She's a lawyer.)

"If they catch you," she said sternly, "they'll lock you up for a very long time."

"Seems to be a family curse," I quipped. Then I told her I was out of options and that the worst they can do to me is nothing compared to what I'd face if I went back to Southeast. I told her I had nothing to lose. She seemed to believe me. No, it was more than that—she seemed to understand. But she insisted on knowing exactly how I got in here. So I asked her if she knew about the Summerhouse.

"Sure, it's on the edge of the Capitol grounds. It was built in the late nineteenth century."

"Eighteen eighty," I said. "By Frederick Olmsted—I looked it up after I moved in."

"¿Y?" Ms. Verita seemed impressed, but she wanted the

details.

"Have you been there?"

"Una sola vez," she said. "Once, and it's beautiful—an oasis in this chaotic corner of the city."

"Well there's a grotto," I said. I felt very reluctant to give away my secret, but I could tell Ms. Verita wasn't going to let me off the hook until she knew. I could also tell that she'd sense a lie real quick. "It was raining. I was cold and tired. So I crawled in. If you crawl in far enough, there's a hatch door that leads to an underground tunnel..." I let my voice trail off. She arched her eyebrows and shook her head.

After that night, I used video surveillance to catch glimpses of Ms. Verita when I could and to engineer the occasional encounter. I got to know her routine. In fact, I looked her up and got to know all about who she works for (House Majority Leader Terry Bridges), what she does (a Legislative Director who writes the bills that Congress votes on), and who's on her staff (even though I've never met them face-to-face, they all seem pretty cool—not like the rest of these stuffed shirts).

As I've said, Ms. Verita's the closest thing I have to a friend around here. She even sneaks me food sometimes, or purposely leaves staff room doors unlocked so I can get supplies.

Just then on the monitor I see Ms. Verita get up and collect her things, which means she's probably heading back to her office since it's getting close to lunchtime. She's the kind of hardworking director who eats her lunch at her desk.

I have to see her today, and not because I have a crush on her, although I would risk venturing out of my suite during the day when Congress is in session for that reason alone. No, over the past couple of days, I came across something that I know she'll find very interesting—troubling, more likely. Because Ms. Verita's boss, Representative Bridges, is the Majority Leader of the House, she's the one responsible for keeping her party in line and making sure that there are enough votes for *her* boss, the Speaker of the House, Representative Robert Landon, to get bills passed. It also means that Representative Bridges is supposed to work directly with the Majority Leader of the Senate— Senator Marcus Charles—to work out deals and compromises so that both the House and the Senate can pass bills.

It's no secret around here that Bridges and Charles don't like each other. It's worse than that; they hate each other like Crips and Bloods. Especially Senator Charles. Ms. Verita says the old goat would stick a bayonet in Bridges if he had the chance. But I don't need Ms. Verita to tell me so. I watch what's going on from my laptop, and ever since I met Ms. Verita and got to know something about her, I've been keeping an eye on Senator Charles. Between me and Rhino, we know everything that goes down in this place, although that might be giving Rhino too much credit.

But, according to Ms. Verita, it's not unusual for Democrats and Republicans to vilify each other. What is unusual is when they're willing to cross the line—break the law—to get their way. And that's what I've discovered with all my slinking around and surveillance: Senator Charles has something up his sleeve that Ms. Verita needs to know about.

I brush my teeth real quick using bottled water and spit into a can. I turn on my webcam one more time to straighten my hair, which mostly means rearranging and pressing flat my tight, curly locks—no hope getting a comb or brush through this mess. I change my T-shirt (I have a few I've snagged from fund-raisers and stuff—could use a new pair of cargo pants, though), and head for the door.

I'm about to leave my suite when I remember the Candy Desk. I flick my laptop back on and bring up a feed of the Senate Chamber. Senators are just beginning to file in for the start of their session. Perfect timing!

I watch as one of the old farts, Senator McElroy, meanders over to the Candy Desk. A smile starts to spread across my face. Everyone knows McElroy by the gold microphone he had installed at his desk in the Senate. I read up about that microphone (because I've been tempted to steal it more than once—it must be worth a fortune). Supposedly, it was a gift from some rich radio talk show host. He gave it to McElroy as a tribute to McElroy standing up during a State of the Union and shouting at the President that he was a schmuck. McElroy was escorted out of the Chamber and later censured by the Senate, but the radio talk show host gave him the microphone, which McElroy promptly installed at his desk in the Senate Chamber. I guess it was his way of flipping the bird at all those senators who voted to censure him.

Another senator stops McElroy right in front of the Candy Desk and begins talking to him. While looking up at the other senator, McElroy reaches into the drawer and blindly pats his hand around. He grabs a couple of "pieces of candy," and hands one to the other senator. When they look down at their hands, they drop what they're holding and let out a simultaneous yell. McElroy stumbles back and is caught by the elbows by other senators who are just making their way up the aisle.

I laugh. The Capitol Kid strikes again! This is better than TV. Rhino's going to be enraged. Satisfied, I flick off my laptop and, with a skip in my step, head off to find Ms. Verita.

By now, I know all the secret tunnels, back stairwells, and service halls running through and under the Capitol complex. The deepest tunnels must have been left after various stages of construction, and the oldest ones were probably secretly dug during the early wars that rolled through here (especially the War of 1812 when the building was burned by the British) so that members of Congress could escape. And the upper service halls and back stairwells were mostly there so slaves and servants could get around unseen. But it's still risky wandering around in the middle of the day, especially when Congress is in session.

I need to get to the Cannon House Office Building, where some of the House staff and aides have offices. Cannon is the oldest of the House Administrative buildings. If you're a senator or congressman or have one of the lead staff positions (like Ms. Verita), you get to take a private subway, which used to be a trolley car, and before that a horse and carriage service, but a while ago I found tunnels that run under the subways. There's one line to serve the Senate side (it stops at all three Senate buildings) and one to the House side. On the House side, the subway only serves one building, Rayburn. Cannon just has a pedestrian walkway, and the other buildings don't get direct service at all. The House always gets the short end of the stick. I'm guessing that there must have been a plan to build a subway to Cannon but for some reason it got scrapped because there's also a tunnel under the pedestrian walkway, and that's what I decide to take now.

The abandoned tunnels I found must have been used during construction of the original trolleys because they look unfinished and are hardly lit. In fact, they were completely dark when I found them, but I replaced a few of the bare, wire-caged bulbs to make it easier to get around. I've never seen anyone down here, not even Rhino's men, and there's no video surveillance.

The problem is getting from the official halls to the underground tunnels without being seen. Every building has different entry points. In the case of Cannon, there's a rusty metal ladder that climbs up through a utility well, which is sealed off by a grate in the back of the building's boiler room—all nice and hidden. The grate is heavy, but with a little WD-40 that I nabbed from the janitors, it slides open more easily. From the boiler room level, I have access to all the stairwells in the building.

Luckily, Ms. Verita's office (359-CHOB) is right at the end of one of the halls on the upper floor of Cannon, so all I have to do is slip across the hall and into her office. What's even luckier is that they did a lousy job installing the security camera (the building was built in 1908) so that it doesn't catch the stairwell door. Unlike the senators' and representatives' offices in the Capitol Building, none of the staff offices have cameras in them, although some of the conference rooms do. For a brief moment, I'll be exposed when I slip into Ms. Verita's office, but it's a chance I'm willing to take.

As soon as the coast is clear, I make my move. I dart across the hall and pause at the door for a moment to listen. Since the security light is green next to the swipe pad, I know she's in there. When I don't hear voices, I figure it's safe, so I open the door and slip inside.

Ms. Verita looks up from her laptop. At first she's startled, then she frowns. She stands and plants her hands on her desk, leaning forward like a stern schoolteacher. She has a yellow cardigan sweater draped over her shoulders that makes her blue dress bluer. My heart thumps.

"Boot! What are you doing here?"

"Saludos, Ms. Verita," I say, using my husky grown up voice.

Ms. Verita shakes her head. "You shouldn't be here. You could—"

She stops herself, stands up straight, then walks around the side of her desk toward me. In a softer tone, she says, "We could both get in trouble. Por favor, cierra la puerta. And please lock it."

It's that soft tone that gets me every time because it's so genuine. Ms. Verita is the only grown-up I know who is able to have a conversation with me on my terms. I can tell that most grown-ups are either distracted when they're talking to me (like my guidance counselor) or don't really want to hear what I have to say even if they pretend to (like LaQuota). But Ms. Verita, she has another gear. She can switch from whatever she's doing to listen—really listen—

to what I have to say. So I try to pay it back whenever I see her. I like to ask her what she's working on, what she's worried about (she always looks worried), and really try to listen. It's one of the reasons I feel like we're friends.

"No one saw me," I say sheepishly, locking the door.

"No seas tonto. You know there are security cameras in the hall," Ms. Verita challenges.

"Your door barely shows up," I say.

Ms. Verita's eyebrows arch. "How do you know?"

I shrug.

"What if someone comes in to see me?"

"It's nearly lunchtime. No one works around here during lunch."

Ms. Verita laughs. "You got me there, Boot. Tienes razón."

I see her relax and take that as my cue that it's OK to stay. At least for a bit. I work my way around her desk and plop into her chair.

Ms. Verita smiles and shakes her head. "Acomódate. Why don't you make yourself comfortable?"

I know she's being sarcastic, but I pretend I don't. "Gracias," I say. I look at her laptop. "What are you working on?"

Ms. Verita sighs and slumps into one of the two visitor chairs positioned on the other side of her desk, the way they are in the principal's office at Ballou STAY (that's my school—when I go). "I don't even know anymore," she says dejectedly. "Ni sé."

I'm about to tell her about Senator Charles when, suddenly, I see her laptop's screen flash. Real quick, like someone pressed the print screen button or like the webcam took a picture. "I think there's something wrong with your computer," I say, turning it sideways so she can see it, but it doesn't flash again.

"What do you mean?"

"I saw the screen flash."

"Oh, it's been acting up lately. I keep meaning to take it down to the IT guys, but I haven't had time."

Without saying anything, I begin typing. I bring up a command shell and start grepping for hidden logs and processes.

"Hey! ¿Qué estás haciendo?" Ms. Verita objects. "What are you doing?" She leans forward to take her laptop back.

"Just a minute," I say. I think I've found something, but Ms. Verita snatches her laptop away from me before I can confirm it.

"That's my property, Boot."

She's angry.

"You have to respect my boundaries."

"I'm sorry, Ms. Verita." I look down at my hands, worried that she might tell me I have to leave.

"I asked you what you were doing," she says, softening her tone. She knows how to handle tough kids.

"I was just searching your files for a trojan." I grin as she raises an eyebrow in surprise. "I'm good with computers," I say, answering her question before she has a chance to ask. "I've been working at this, um, shop for the last five years, uh, restoring computers and smartphones."

Ms. Verita frowns, because she knows I'm lying about something, but I can tell she's also impressed. It's the gleam in her eyes that gives her away.

"And why do you think I have a trojan on my

computer?"

I reach my hand out to gesture that I can show her. Slowly, she hands me the laptop.

With a few more commands, I find what I'm looking for. It's labeled just like a Microsoft utility, but it's not the usual customer.

"Who are you communicating with?" I mutter to the trojan.

By now, Ms. Verita is leaning over my shoulder with a mixed look on her face. She's speechless, concerned, and angry all at once. And she smells so good. It's not perfume or anything, it's just her. I almost lose focus, but it would be too embarrassing, so I swallow hard and glance up at her nervously.

Ms. Verita misinterprets my glance. She thinks I think she doesn't know what I'm doing. "I took a Web Design and Coding class in college," she says a little defensively. "I can hold my own with HTML and CSS."

I arch my eyebrows and nod, but don't say anything. HTML and CSS have nothing to do with operating system trojans or tunneling through VPNs, but I don't want her to think I'm judging her.

I suspect that the rogue virus is designed to take a picture of Ms. Verita's screen at periodic intervals, which would explain the desktop flashing. Using a print screen function or accessing peripherals like a webcam or microphone is simpler than loading a more sophisticated program to search through files and registries. Plus, you get to see what the user is working on—emails, chat, documents, browsers, spreadsheets, everything—with one little command…as long as it doesn't get noticed.

I decide to turn on a network trace and, just as I have it up and running, the screen blinks again. Perfect. My trace picks up the process ID and moments later I have a local IP address indicating where the snapshots are being sent. Whoever's tapped into Ms. Verita's laptop doesn't want to leave evidence on her machine other than the offending trojan. I log in to the account I created on the Congressional VPN, and look up the IP address. The whole time, Ms. Verita is entranced, but she also seems to be following me.

"Julien," she whispers when an office number, SR-322, comes up in a table next to the IP address. "Senator Charles's Chief of Staff."

I sit back and fold my arms. "Looks like Senator Charles wants to know what you're up to," I say. Then I wink and add, "Or else Julien has the hots—"

"¡Ya basta!" Ms. Verita interrupts with a scowl. "That's enough. It's also disgusting." She shakes her head and hands like she's been sullied by the thought of Julien.

"It's pretty interesting, Ms. Verita," I say, "that Senator Charles's Chief of Staff is monitoring you."

"What do you mean?" Ms. Verita looks alarmed. "What else do you know?"

"Bueno," I say, smirking like I'm a trial lawyer pointing to undeniable evidence. "I think we've established that I'm pretty good with computers. Helps me keep tabs on things and stay a step ahead of Rhino and his gang." I grin, but Ms. Verita isn't in the mood.

She folds her arms and scowls. "Why do you think Julien spying on me is 'interesting,' Boot?"

I clear my throat. "Because he's not just spying on other

politicians. He's bribing them, too."

"Bribing?" she says. "That's a serious charge. How do you know?"

I raise my hands, palms out, as if to surrender. "Hey, I'm just a street kid," I remind her, grinning. "But when one guy hands another guy an envelope stuffed with cash…even a street kid knows what's going down."

"¿Pero y tú lo viste? ¿Dónde?"

Ms. Verita slips exclusively into Spanish only when she's really worked up.

"Yo te dije, it pays for a—uh—special hotel guest like me to keep an eye on things. Helps me maintain my VIP status." I wink.

Ms. Verita glares at me until I feel uncomfortable. "I want to know everything," she says, speaking slowly.

"What do you mean?"

"I mean, how did you just do that?" She points to her laptop. "And how do you know about a bribe?"

I shrug. "OK. Want me to delete the trojan?"

"Yes. Wait—no!" Ms. Verita says. She begins to pace.

She stops and turns slowly to face me. "No, Boot," she says quietly, "I have another idea. That is, if you're willing to help me."

My heart melts into my gut. Of course I'm willing to help her. I'd do just about anything for Ms. Verita! She must see how I'm feeling, because she smiles at me like a goddess.

THE DUMMIES ACT

After a couple of months snooping around the Capitol and spying on its patrons, I thought I had these pampered politicians pegged. They're like celebrities: rich, spoiled, and full of themselves. But it turns out I don't know the half of it—not by a long shot—to hear Ms. Verita describe the way senators and representatives bribe and blackmail one another (my words; she used *entice* and *induce*).

Honestly, I didn't know anything about politics or national news until I moved in here, and I had no reason to think much about them. I was just trying to survive day by day. But here, you can't avoid politics, for obvious reasons. All day long you hear words and phrases like *partisan* and *other side of the aisle* (that one makes me think of a wedding). And all the offices have flat screens and they're all tuned to one cable news station or another so the politicians can watch themselves like they're studying game replays between halves.

It's like they all go to the same boot camp because as soon as a video camera gets stuck in their faces, every one of them knows how to turn on their Capitol Charm (that's with a Capitol *C*) to enchant the audience. Some are better at it than others. And they all know they're doing it, too.

To me, it's like watching a magic show. You know you're being tricked, but you're willing to watch over and over again anyway because it's fun to see the impossible. When these magicians have their Capitol Charm turned way up high, they could be saying one thing while doing exactly the opposite and hardly anyone would notice. How do I know? I hear them joke about it among themselves. I even heard one guy call his practiced smiles and righteous tones "political fairy dust."

But everyone knows that a lot of the thrill of a magic show comes from the anticipation that the magician might slip up. If that happens, his trick gets exposed.

In the case of Congress, the really brazen mistakes have a way of becoming national news. Like that time the smiling, bronzed senator from Arizona got caught bribing someone to hide incriminating evidence about his past. He kept telling reporters that he didn't do anything wrong, until finally someone posted an anonymous video on YouTube that showed him laughing about his crime with some friends. Even then his Capitol Charm almost got him out of it. Almost. In the end, he resigned.

It's not just the politicians, either; the staffers around here have learned to use Capitol Charm, too. I know this because I catch glimpses of what gets said and done behind closed doors.

That's how I saw one of Senator Charles's staffers hand

a big fat envelope full of cash to another staffer. (I didn't actually see the cash, but judging by the shape it was either a brick or a stack of bills.) Don't they realize how much surveillance there is around this place? To me, it was surprising and kind of funny to see two guys all dressed up in business suits breaking the law like that. At least Stang and his crew look and talk like criminals. Oh, they might smile at you and agree to do something, but at least you know when they're coming to stab you in the back it's with an actual knife.

By the time I leave Ms. Verita's office, my head is spinning from everything I've just learned about how this place really works. I'm also on cloud nine because Ms. Verita gave me her phone number! I mean, I already knew it—she doesn't know I knew it—but now she actually gave it to me. She wants me to figure out a few things for her and then give her a call. She also said that a smart teen like me ought to be in school. She was using that soft, seductive, I-can-relate-to-you voice of hers. Her version of Capitol Charm. She convinced me to tell her how I got my computer experience working for LaQuota and Dottie.

I almost told her the rest of my story, too…almost. But I didn't want her to feel sorry for me; I hate it when people give you that look like you're some kind of helpless charity case. I used to get that all the time when my parents gave me the boot and I had to sleep under a bench or grab some newspapers because I was cold. But I feel in my heart that I want to tell Ms. Verita everything, and that makes me happier than I've been in a long time.

But what's really on my mind as I slip back into the

stairwell across the hall is what Ms. Verita told me about the showdown coming in Congress. It's a showdown, she claimed, for the history books. A showdown that started when the Civil War ended.

At first I thought she was joking. I mean, the Civil War ended—what—more than a hundred and fifty years ago?

I said as much to her, and started to laugh because she seemed so dramatic. She frowned at me and planted her hands on her hips. She told me to go right on laughing, but that I was proof the Civil War never really ended. That made me listen up.

She explained that the struggle just shifted from white supremacy to rich supremacy (her words)—that the battle lines were redrawn from black and white to rich and poor (which, she said, conveniently includes a disproportionate number of minorities). She said that instead of *military* companies blowing each other up on battlefields with rifles and cannonballs, today it's *corporate* companies hurling money at politicians to buy their votes.

But that's just the backdrop for what's been happening in Congress. If I understood her correctly, this historic struggle is coming to a head. There are two competing bills that Congress is considering passing before the end of the year. The House of Representatives—including Representative Bridges and Ms. Verita—has written one of the bills. It's called Democracy First. The Senate—including Senator Charles and Julien Landreau, Senator Charles's Chief of Staff, aka the guy we think is spying on Ms. Verita—has written the other. Their bill is called Real Reform, but everyone working for Representative Bridges calls it "The Dummies Act."

So it's Democracy First versus The Dummies Act.

I know, it doesn't sound so terrible. Not like Godzilla versus King Kong or anything, but, well, that's Capitol Charm for you.

Before I moved in here, I never knew how laws were made in our fair land, but hanging around this place, you can't help but learn a thing or two. I mean, I knew that there are three branches of government: Legislative for making laws (that's Congress); Judicial for interpreting laws (that's the courts); and Executive for enforcing laws (that's the President). And most people know there are two chambers in Congress: the House of Representatives and the Senate.

But I never really knew how a law actually got made.

When Ms. Verita started explaining the competing bills to me, I had to stop her. I didn't really want her to know that *I* didn't know what she was talking about. But I also knew I wasn't going to be able to help her if I didn't understand what was going on.

"Está bien, Boot," Ms. Verita said in her warm, instructive tone. "Most politicians around here don't know, either." She laughed. "They rely on their staff."

Ms. Verita took off her pretty yellow sweater at that point, sat on the edge of her desk, and started swinging her legs as she explained it to me.

"It's like this, Boot. A bill is just a new law, and it can start from anywhere or anyone, including you or me. Let's say we want to make changes to our schools, not just locally, but across the whole nation. What we have to do is convince the politicians—senators or representatives in

Congress—who represent us to propose a new law that will implement those changes. If they're convinced, they have their staffs create a draft of the changes we want in the form of a bill. The draft is then reviewed by the committee that oversees that area. There are committees for everything, like Energy or Agriculture or Transportation. In fact, both the House and the Senate have about twenty committees each, although they don't all have the exact same names.

"So if you want to make a change to schools, Boot, an Education Committee would review it. Once the committee makes its changes and approves it, the rest of that Chamber—that means either the House or Senate—votes on it. If it gets a majority, then the bill goes to the other Chamber, and they vote on it, too. If it passes the second Chamber, then it goes to the President to sign."

If Ms. Verita was my teacher, I wouldn't miss a day of school. "Sounds pretty simple," I told her.

She nodded. "It is...when everything's working smoothly. The problem comes in when really rich people and corporations want Congress to pass only laws that help them or the causes they believe in. They're called *special interests*, and they hire lobbyists—in the old days, lobbyists were people who used to stand in the Capitol lobby and try to convince congressmen to vote one way or another, but it's become much more sophisticated. In fact, it's a whole industry. Very lucrative, too. Nowadays, lobbyists use discreet tactics to bribe politicians to get their way. They also pay off the media to report things in a way that makes them look good—that's called spin. The effect of all that bribing and spinning is to rig the laws in the special interest's favor and to trick ordinary people into thinking that it's good for them, too, when it's really not."

I can understand bribes and spin. They're part of the magic show. It's what Stang and his crew do, too. They make everyone in our nabe think they're the ones keeping the peace—handing out cash to protect the neighborhood from other crews and gangs and crooked cops. But they're really just screwing us all over so they can sell their drugs and control the streets.

"The goal of Democracy First," Ms. Verita went on proudly, "is to restore our democracy by giving power back to ordinary people and taking it away from really rich people and corporations—I call them Rich Supremacists—who want to stay in control, just like white plantation owners did in the nineteenth century.

"Our bill has three main parts to it. The first is to provide more money for public education so that schools can build more classrooms, hire more teachers, and reduce class sizes to something manageable. With a better education, ordinary people will have more opportunities and will be smarter voters. And the smarter they are, the more confident they are. And the more confident they are, Boot, the stronger their voice.

"The second part of our bill puts limits on how much rich people and corporations can give to politicians. That will limit the influence of special interests. The third part is to require the media to publicly distinguish between news and spin."

I followed Ms. Verita's explanation, but Democracy First sounded like a pretty ambitious bill with lots of changes. Then again, what do I know about making new laws?

"The goal of the other bill, Real Reform," Ms. Verita went on, "is to do just the opposite. It's to make sure that Rich Supremacists remain in control of our democracy forever. But Real Reform is sneaky. On the surface, it looks like its education goals are similar to Democracy First's by allocating lots of money to public schools. Only, in the case of Real Reform, there are two essential differences. First, the money is not coming from government, it's coming from big corporations who agree to be sponsors—kind of like the way that big corporations pay money to put their names on stadiums, only in this case they'll be putting their names on schools."

"Oh, like FedEx Field."

"¡Exactamente! Except your high school would be called FedEx High."

I shrugged. "Doesn't sound so bad to me. Although, I'd want Under Armour sponsoring my school," I teased. "I could use some free stuff."

Ms. Verita frowned. "On the surface, it doesn't seem bad. Especially since everyone is used to seeing corporate names splashed across everything. But if The Dummies Act passes, it will be what happens *inside* the schools that's the second, bigger problem.

"Imagine going to school in the morning, sitting in class for maybe an hour, just long enough so that you can learn to read and write, and then spending the rest of your day working for the company that's sponsoring your school—starting in the fourth grade. No history, no math, no science, no sports, no music, no art, no clubs, nothing but the bare minimum."

"Do I get paid?"

"Boot!" Ms. Verita snapped. "You might get paid something, but it wouldn't be a living wage. Worse, if Under Armour sponsored your school, you wouldn't be learning anything except how to stitch underwear together."

"What about Apple or Microsoft? Maybe if they sponsored my school, I'd learn how to write more software."

"No, you wouldn't. Those jobs require advanced mathematics and computer-science skills, which would be saved for private-school kids. All you would know how to do is slap protective plastic on a smartphone and stuff it in a box for shipping. You would have no hope of doing anything else with your life. You'd be nothing more than a slave!" I could tell that Real Reform made Ms. Verita's blood boil.

She said that Senator Charles's dastardly plan is to convert public schools into work houses for poor and middle-class kids who can't afford private school.

The phrase *work houses* triggered something I remembered seeing in Disney's *A Christmas Carol*. "You mean like what Scrooge tells the charity workers about work houses for the poor." I grinned at her. "Senator Scrooge."

She laughed at that, but only briefly before getting serious again. She called it a power play by the rich that will provide cheap labor for their corporations who will look like they're generously donating money. But they'll actually make a profit on all those low-wage student workers. According to Ms. Verita, the sponsors of Real Reform claim they'll be giving people who can't afford a good education (like me) a valuable skill at an early age. Now that's Capitol Charm.

But Ms. Verita said the effect would be to make poor and middle-class people less educated and less skilled than rich people, which means they'll remain poor forever.

That's why she calls it The Dummies Act.

Based on what Ms. Verita explained and what I've learned on my own since I've been here, it seems to me that ever since the days when Brooks beat Sumner nearly to death, it's never really been about black and white, but more about Haves and Have Nots. And it seems that politicians have always been divided into two warring camps—those who represent the Haves (my simple term for Ms. Verita's Rich Supremacists), and those who represent the Have Nots (everyone else).

Ms. Verita says that TVs, computers, the Internet, and all that modern technology has only made the conflict worse because now the two camps can act faster and be more clandestine. Just like that guy, Julien, who's using a trojan virus to figure out what Ms. Verita is up to. In the old days, what Julien is doing would have required sending a spy into Representative Bridges's camp—someone working undercover. Only now, the spy is a small, executable file hidden among millions of other executable files on a computer. It's harder to trace, and if you catch it, you can't torture it for information. Well, that's not entirely true—and that's where I come in.

My homework is to figure out exactly what the trojan on Ms. Verita's computer does and how long it's been doing it. I told Ms. Verita no sweat, which was partially true and partially bragging. I know I can figure out all the things the virus does—I already have my suspicions. But when it comes to figuring out how long it's been on her machine—that might require a little midnight sleuthing across enemy lines. I didn't tell Ms. Verita that—she already told me not to do anything that could get me in any more trouble with the law than I already am just by being a stowaway here. But as I've said before, the alternative is to give up, return home, and face Stang. He's going to kill me. Juvie would be better than that.

Just before I left her office, Ms. Verita said sternly, "I don't want you going anywhere near Julien or Senator Charles." When I nodded offhandedly, she added, and this time her voice sounded surprisingly cold, "I mean it, Boot. They'll be able to connect you with me even if you don't talk. People around here know about you. You will compromise everything for us if they catch you." Now *that* was heavy. Ms. Verita almost sounded mean, which is out of character for her. But she made her point, and I have a feeling that's going to create a problem for me.

"**Got** you now, kid!" Melon says, leaping out from behind one of the columns in The Crypt. I must have been daydreaming and taken a wrong turn out of the service hall, because I know better than to walk openly down the main corridors even on the lower level, especially during the day, and especially when Congress is in session.

Lucky for me, Melon leaped too soon, plus he announced himself before he had me throttled. I squirm away from him, tearing the collar of my T-shirt, and take off, darting between the densely packed columns and arches. This place is called The Crypt because it sits below the Rotunda, like those somber stony chambers that lie beneath the main floor of a church. Some say George Washington was buried beneath The Crypt, but I've looked it up and supposedly he's still buried in Mt. Vernon. But it sure looks like somebody could be buried under here.

I get lucky twice this afternoon, because, not only did Melon miss me on his first attempt, but The Crypt, which is normally busy with staffers and aides and tourists passing back and forth, is empty. It's lunchtime and no one seems to be around, which makes me wonder what Melon was doing down here. It's not like the guards to set a trap for me during the day. Probably just coincidence. But I still don't know how I let myself wander out in the open. One minute I was walking down the dim passage under the Cannon pedestrian walkway, and the next I was in The Crypt. Must still be under Ms. Verita's spell.

"You won't get away, kid!" Melon shouts, but I know he can't see me, and by the sound of his voice, I've got the lead on him. I slip in behind the statue of John C. Calhoun and think I have Melon fooled. I wait a few minutes, hear him shuffling around, then nothing. There are, however, voices echoing, which means someone's heading this way. I take that as my cue, but just as I step out from the shadow of Calhoun, Melon steps out from the nearest column, sneering. He has me cornered and he knows it.

He's about to say something gleeful when I start to run at him, full speed. I see his eyebrows arch in surprise, then he spreads his legs, just as I'd hoped, to absorb the blow of me hitting him. Instead, I slide on the polished marble floor, right between his legs, leap to my feet on the other side, and take off at a full sprint. Now I know I'm safe.

"Maybe next time, Melon!" I call. I can hear his gear clanking and clattering as he takes off after me, but I'm already entering a service door. I bound down a few steps, jump out into the subbasement, which is luckily a maze of passages, and disappear. I don't stop trotting until I'm back to my suite.

That was too close.

TROJAN WARS

*I*t's midnight before I finally figure out all the things Julien's trojan is doing to Ms. Verita's laptop. It's a fancy bugging application. It activates her webcam and microphone, and streams the feedback to an anonymous server that I'm guessing is in Julien's office. Probably a network server he has hidden somewhere in a closet or under his desk. It also takes snapshots of her desktop, which, as I'd guessed, was the source of the flashing.

But to figure out how long Charles's gang has been spying on Bridges's gang, I need to get into Julien's office and jack in to that server directly. He's got a pretty good firewall up around it that I can't seem to get past, which means I'll have to do it the hand-to-hand combat way (by plugging into his server directly).

I check the surveillance streams of the Russell office building. It's much busier than usual for this time of night—all those politicians demanding instant service from their staff—but Julien's office seems to be quiet. Almost too quiet, considering he's the Chief of Staff for the Majority Leader of the Senate.

I know it's risky to go over there, but I really want to impress Ms. Verita. I'd also like to poke my finger in Senator Charles's eye, and busting into his Chief of Staff's office to steal some things off their secret server seems like a good way to do it. Julien also has an office next to Senator Charles's luxurious suite in the Capitol Building, but I've learned that all the action takes place in these administrative office buildings. The Capitol is mostly for pomp and ceremony, although Representative Bridges does tend to have working sessions in her conference rooms. It's one of the things I like about her.

I grab some cables—USB, FireWire, and Ethernet—just to make sure I get connected, and the little black box I bought off the Internet. I call it Black Beauty. This sweet gadget allows me to hack into anything. Anywhere there's a public Wi-Fi, I can sit there with my laptop and Black Beauty and intercept every single device accessing that Wi-Fi.

Black Beauty has a transceiver and its own ISP connection so it piggybacks on the local Wi-Fi and tricks all the devices into connecting with it. It does this by snatching preferred network names from each device and broadcasting those back to them. Each device thinks it's connecting to a preferred network like Home or Office, which means it thinks it's secure. Once all the traffic is flowing through Black Beauty, I can pick up user IDs, passwords, names…everything.

I like to play a game sometimes where I'll sit in a public

place like the Francis A. Gregory Library on Alabama Avenue and see how fast I can get the names, IDs, and passwords of all the people connected. Then I Google them to match the names with faces. Sometimes I walk out of the library knowing half the people there by name, where they live, work, and I have their IDs and sometimes their passwords, too. If I was a real crook, I would sell that data or use it myself to empty bank accounts, open credit cards—you name it. People can be clueless. They get mugged blind every day and don't even know it.

But the power of Black Beauty doesn't stop there. I can also jack it directly into a server and it will find all of the ports and connected IP addresses and then open a port for me, mimicking a secure IP address. That way I look like a legit connection. The box cost me $39.99 online, which is a lot for me, but it was worth it.

I stuff Black Beauty and my laptop into one of my makeshift backpacks (canvas bag with rope and homemade pull string) along with the master key card I swiped from one of Rhino's guards, and head out. The hall seems darker than usual, which reminds me it might be a good idea to grab a flashlight, so I double back to get one. As I'm about to close the door, I see an old pizza box in the corner. I grab that and my baseball cap, then head out again.

When Congress is in session, there are several pizza places and diners that deliver twenty-four hours a day, so it's not a bad disguise. I've snagged a few disguises, like a waiter's outfit for the Senate Dining Room, a janitor uniform, and a security guard shirt (all of Rhino's guys are so big, the guard shirt doesn't fit me, and Chase's would be too busty).

By the time I reach the Russell building, it's nearly 1:00 a.m. I'm hoping that things have died down a bit upstairs. My adrenaline's pumping, so I take the metal stairs two at a time. I know I'm passing the main floor when the stairs turn to gray-painted concrete. Julien's office is on the third floor.

There's nobody in the hall when I peek through the stairwell door, but I know that the video surveillance camera will see me. I've come prepared. I put on my baseball cap and hold the pizza box flat, like it's got a fresh, hot pie in it.

I stroll down the hall and knock on Julien's door. When no one answers, I try the knob. Locked! No problem. I turn my back to the camera and use the pizza box to block what I'm doing. I've got the guard's key card, which can open any door in this place by pressing it against the keypad on the door. But I'm nervous, and I hear voices down the hall, which makes me jittery. Of course I drop the card.

I swear under my breath and then bend down carefully to hide what I'm doing. A few seconds later, I've got the key card pressed against the pad. A light flashes from red to green and the knob turns. I try to make it look like someone's answered the door, but I know that if any of the guards scrutinize the surveillance streams, they'll figure out what's going on. Luckily, I remembered to disable the security camera in Julien's office before coming over here (figures that he's one of the self-important staffers who would have a camera installed *inside* his office, just like his boss), but it was too risky to take out the hall cameras, too. I just have to hope they have no reason to go back and look at the feeds.

As soon as I'm in Julien's office, I drop the pizza box and my baseball cap on the nearest chair, lock the door, and take inventory, using my flashlight rather than the overhead lights. The first thing I notice is that his office is nearly twice the size of Ms. Verita's, and furnished with a plush sofa, two lounge chairs, and a large, flat-screen TV. I don't know why, but it irritates me that Julien is better compensated than Ms. Verita. Her job is no less important than his, and she's a much nicer person. I hear the voice of my mother in my head, "Ay m'ijo, la vida no es justa. Son, life isn't fair, and once you get that in your head, you'll be much happier."

Remembering my mother's lame advice irritates me more. Life may not be fair, but that doesn't mean I have to lie down and accept it—or smoke heroin like she does to sugarcoat it.

Muttering under my breath, I begin looking around Julien's office, which is pretty cluttered. It won't be easy to find the server, but my guess is that it's wired, not wireless, so I decide to start looking for Ethernet jacks. There's plenty of gear on his desk—two monitors, a laptop that's locked to the desk leg, wireless keyboard and mouse, GOgroove speakers, and more…but no server. I begin shuffling through the deep drawers in his desk. Nothing.

Just then, I hear voices in the hall. I freeze and begin combing the room for a hiding place. That's when I notice the louvered Murphy bed doors in the corner. I'm skinny; maybe I could slip in between the bed and the doors. Luckily, the voices pass, but I notice green-and-yellow diode lights flashing through the louvers of the Murphy bed closet.

"Gotcha!" I whisper in triumph, getting up and crossing the room.

Sure enough, there's no bed; it's been refurbished into a hardware closet. There's more than one server in here. Looks to me like Senator Charles is bugging the whole freaking Congress with all this gear. But these blades are all connected along a single chassis, which means that if I tap into one, I'll have access to all of them. I decide Ethernet is my best option. I pull out Black Beauty, plug her into the server and my laptop, then boot up.

I hold the flashlight between my teeth and get to work. A few minutes later, I'm in. It takes me a little while to figure out Julien's filing system, but he's got his little spy network running on Linux, which is easier to search through than Windows, so it doesn't take me long to find files associated with Bridges. Along the way, I realize that he really is bugging half of Congress. There are terabytes worth of surveillance here: video, audio, and desktop jpeg images, just like Ms. Verita's. I want to copy all of it, but my laptop has only three hundred gigs available. I'm mad at myself. I should have thought to bring the portable Passport hard drive I swiped last month from a staffer's office (don't even know which one). It holds two terabytes, and I could have grabbed a whole bunch of these files. But another idea occurs to me. I search through my own files and find what I'm looking for. It's my own homemade trojan. Not as sophisticated as Julien's. It doesn't bug or record anything, but it will find the user admin tables on Julien's network and FTP them to me at a later time. It might take a little while to do its job—like hours—but if it works, I'll have all the IDs and passwords I need to get past Julien's firewall and snag the rest of his illicit computer taps.

For now, I make sure I copy all of the Bridges files (which go back nearly six months, although it looks like there are a lot more files logged in the past two), and begin copying some of the others whose names I'm familiar with. There's the Speaker of the House, Landon, and the Minority Leader in the Senate, Oppenheimer. That's when I run out of space.

It's also when I run out of luck.

I hear voices in the hall again. This time, they stop in front of Julien's door. I flick off the flashlight and close the lid on my laptop.

There's room beneath the bottom shelf in the hardware closet, if I can fold myself into it quickly enough. I'm easing the Murphy door closed just as the lights flick on in the office. There are two people coming in, Julien and a lady friend.

The pizza box! I start to sweat. No way Julien won't notice the pizza box sitting on the chair. Sure enough, it's the first thing out of his mouth.

"Who left—" Julien starts to say. His voice is angry, but he checks his temper. I can tell he's turned on his Capitol Charm, because his voice turns husky as he says to his friend, "That's what you get for letting interns use your office."

I hear the pizza box land on the floor near the garbage can.

"Can I fix you a drink?" he asks. His voice is nasally, his tone affected. I can tell the guy is high on himself. I already don't like him because of what he's been doing to

Ms. Verita, but to hear him speak just confirms it.

"Sure. What do you have?" his friend says. Her voice is perky. I can see through the slats in the louver doors that she's wearing a snug crimson dress, thigh high, no shoulder straps.

"Single malt and single malt," Julien says, chuckling.

His lady friend laughs. "I'll take single malt. Do you have any rocks?"

"Of course I do. The Senate is the five-star side of this hotel! You'd be drinking cheap Black Label beer on the House side," Julien jokes.

The lady laughs again. "Julien!"

I hear him open the door to his mini fridge, followed by the clink of some cubes. I grimace. Ms. Verita's comments about Rich Supremacists seem to be playing out in real time.

A few minutes later, they're sitting on the couch, drinking Scotch and watching the big TV. At least with the background noise, I can move my leg, which has fallen asleep and is starting to hurt.

I can't see the couch from where I am, but I don't need to. Pretty soon, I can tell what Julien and his friend are doing is not PG-13.

After a while, both my legs start throbbing and my crunched neck hurts, but I can't move because the sounds from the couch have died down.

I figure they'll fall asleep in a bit, which might give me a chance to sneak out, but then I hear Julien stir. Suddenly, he's all business.

"You know, Lana, I should warn you, now that Congress is back in session, the rest of this week is going to be very long. If you have any plans, cancel them. We're going to be working around the clock."

"What's new," Lana says sarcastically. "You know, Julien, I might not have signed on to be your administrative assistant if you'd told me about the hours." She laughs. But then she says in a more serious tone, "What's so special about this week? I figured it would be a light one leading up to Thanksgiving."

"We've confirmed that Bridges is planning to bring Democracy First to the floor of the House on Friday. She wants to spring one on Senator Charles right before Congress takes off for Thanksgiving break. But we're a few steps ahead of her. She thinks she can whip the vote—and her Democratic colleagues will tell her yes—but we have enough votes that will turn on her at the last minute. Charles has Speaker Landon by the short hairs." He snickers. I hear him get up from the couch and start pacing the room.

"As soon as Bridges's bill fails, Landon will introduce Real Reform on the House floor, which, with the votes we've managed to acquire, will pass by a narrow margin. After that, it will sail through the Senate. And the President has already indicated he'll sign it as long as it has provisions to reduce the national debt. Bridges will be humiliated. It will be the end of her short, pitiful run as Majority Leader. More importantly, it will be the beginning of a new and prosperous era in America."

"Which congressmen did you blackmail?" Lana asks, laughing nervously.

"I prefer to see it as loyalty," Julien says. His tone sounds indignant. "Loyalty to Senator Charles and all that the great man has stood for. It's a shame that this will have to be his last term, but he intends to make it his most meaningful, and he's happy to call in all the debts he's owed."

"Oh, Julien, do we have to discuss this now? Come on back to the couch and snuggle with me."

Julien ignores Lana. He sits down at his desk and begins typing on his keyboard. I can see him through the louvers. He's shorter than his official photo makes him look, but he has that chiseled chin, square jaw, and, even after his romp on the couch, perfectly combed hair. Must take a lot of spray to keep it that tight.

"You're not going to start working now," Lana complains.

"You can go," Julien says—a command, not a request. "Tomorrow is Wednesday. That means we have two days to make sure everything is in place."

Lana harrumphs. I hear her gather her things. When she walks over to the desk, I can see her through the slats. Suddenly, I feel sorry for her. And even though I don't like Julien, I have a good feeling about Lana. Call it street instinct. Maybe she could help me and Ms. Verita. *Or maybe you just have the hots for her, Boot.* I feel my face flush, followed by this strange feeling that I've betrayed Ms. Verita for even thinking about Lana. Sometimes I frustrate myself with my twisted logic.

Lana finishes making herself presentable, then pecks Julien on the cheek. He brushes her off. She harrumphs again, and says, "Thanks for dinner, Julien." She pauses, then coos, "And everything else." She has her Capitol Charm on.

Julien grunts, but doesn't look up from his laptop.

Hiding her frustration, Lana spins on her spiky heels and lets herself out.

It's down to me and Julien. Part of me wants to leap out of this closet and strangle the jerk. But I know that now's not the time. I've got to figure out how to get out of here with the evidence I have. Besides, I'm not leaping anywhere at the moment. My legs are so numb, they're almost paralyzed.

Julien pecks away at his keyboard for another fifteen minutes before calling it quits. He yawns, stretches, then plops his feet up on his desk facing the TV. I get a good look at him: alabaster skin, *GQ* hair, tailored suit. He has that polished rich kid aura, like he's used to everything going his way…like someone who has a lot to lose.

I smile to myself. I'll bet Julien's never had to deal with a street kid, with someone who has nothing to lose.

After flicking around the channels for a few minutes, Julien yawns again. He gets up, shuts off the lights, and leaves his office.

As soon as the door closes, I let out a big sigh and tumble out of the closet. I lie there for several minutes, then start slapping my thighs to bring them back to life. When I think my legs are steady enough to walk again, I grab my baseball cap from the chair (funny that Julien never noticed it), peek out of the door, and make a dash for the stairwell.

That last dash is going to be on the video surveillance stream, but I just have to hope that fate is on my side, and that it will be overlooked—now and in the future.

By the time I get back to my suite, I'm beat. I fall onto my cot and crash, not even bothering to take off my backpack. An image from a book on Greek mythology comes to mind. I remember it from fourth grade. A big white horse on wheels being rolled through the gates of unsuspecting Troy. Before I drift off, I think to myself, *Let the Trojan Wars begin.*

REPRESENTATIVE BRIDGES

When I open my eyes, it feels late, even though I have no way to tell other than my various electronic devices. There's no sun down here in my subterranean suite. I panic—I know I need to contact Ms. Verita to let her know about Senator Charles's plan to sabotage the House vote this week. Two days. That's all she has to stop Senator Charles and Julien. The good news is, I'm pretty sure I have the evidence she needs to stop them.

My bag is still strapped to my back, so I pull it off and plug in my laptop. As it's booting up, the night I spent in Julien's closet starts coming back in vivid detail. Then it occurs to me that I can't tell Ms. Verita any of it, because she specifically told me not to go near Julien or Senator Charles. How am I going to tell her I spent half the night in Julien's office?

I frown and rub sleep from my eyes with the backs of my knuckles.

As soon as my laptop's live, I bring up a command shell and check my trojan's log file. It's already sent me a system admin ID and password, and has left an open socket on Julien's server to connect. I smile—two can play this game.

I plug in the Passport hard drive I lifted from one of the staff rooms, and plug it into my laptop. Then I launch PuTTY (a telnet and SSH client that gives me access to a remote server), and log in to Julien's. As soon as I'm connected, I begin downloading the rest of the files that I'd found last night.

While that's running, I finish emptying my backpack, and that's when it hits me: Black Beauty is missing! I feel the blood drain from my face, because I remember exactly where I left it.

I fall back onto my cot.

I unplugged so fast when I heard voices in the hall that I left it sitting on the shelf next to Julien's server. And I forgot all about it while I lay crunched up like a sardine under the shelf.

I panic.

As soon as somebody sees it, they'll know what happened. I swear at myself. Now I really don't know what to do!

Think, Boot, think!

I bang the heel of my hand against my forehead, as if it will jar loose a brilliant solution. But I know it won't. I screwed up. It's that simple. Once they discover Black Beauty, they'll check the surveillance tapes from Julien's office and see that they were suspiciously disabled. Then they'll look at the ones from the hall outside his office. And once they check those, they'll see a pizza boy breaking in…

I groan and curl up into a ball on my cot.

I lie there for a while, but nothing comes to me. I'm feeling sorry for myself, and not thinking clearly. If Ms. Verita finds out, she'll never speak to me again. I violated what tentative trust there was between us. I groan some more. A tear escapes from the corner of my eye.

At last, I sit up. There's only one thing for me to do. I have to get back into Julien's office tonight. *You have nothing to lose, Boot,* I remind myself. But I know it's just a con. I have Ms. Verita to lose.

Just then, my laptop beeps. The download is finished. It gives me a thought. As long as my trojan's running, I'll know Julien's server is live. And as long as it's live, I'll know they haven't found Black Beauty. Suddenly, that trojan is like a beacon in the dark.

But I also have to figure out how to tell Ms. Verita about Julien's plot. I need to think up a good lie. At least until I cover my tracks.

While I'm thinking about what to tell Ms. Verita (or, really, to put off thinking about it), I sit down in front of my laptop and start looking through the files, curious to see what Julien's got on all these politicians.

I go to the folder labeled *Bridges* and open it. It's filled with MPEGs and JPEGs. The MPEGs have the video and audio from the webcam and mike, and the JPEGs have the images of Ms. Verita's desktop.

I randomly click one of the MPEGs dated a couple of days ago. When it starts running, I'm confused. This is not Ms. Verita's office. It's much too elaborate, like some fancy ballroom. I hear Representative Bridges speaking, but I see Ms. Verita's face. She's looking down at her keyboard.

Then I realize that this is a laptop, which means it travels, which means it's picked up video and audio from all over the Capitol Building—wherever Ms. Verita takes it, even to her home. It makes me angry to think that they might have been spying on Ms. Verita in her own home, but I have to admit, I'm curious, too.

"I don't know, Lucy," Representative Bridges is saying to Ms. Verita. "Charles has us boxed in."

"Yes," Ms. Verita responds (the webcam is pointing straight at her chest; she's wearing a calico dress covered by a white cardigan), "but you know that if we get the vote in the House, Oppenheimer says she has enough conservatives in the Senate who have agreed to cross over and support Democracy First."

"I know, but I'm worried, Lucy. Charles and his cronies are spinning our bill as a depraved play on words. They're calling it the end of democracy in America. They're trying to equate passing Democracy First with bankrupting the American dream, when, in truth, it's their bill—that damned Dummies Act—that will bankrupt education. It's the most bald-faced doublespeak I've ever seen, but the media seems to be biting."

"But Terry, you know it's all propaganda," Ms. Verita counters. Her voice is strong and convincing. "The media is on Charles's side because our bill strips *news* status from all of the major cable networks." Ms. Verita puts air quotes around the word *news* with her fingers.

"Yes, and Newscorp has pulled out all the stops to slander our bill as a result," Representative Bridges replies unhappily. "Murdoch's office has been calling me 24-7. Comcast is threatening to sue. CNN is calling it an outrage.

Maybe we should reconsider—"

"No, Terry!" Ms. Verita raises her voice uncharacteristically. "As it is, we've agreed to drop campaign finance limits from our bill, which would restrict the influence of lobbyists and special interests."

At this, I can hear Representative Bridges chuckle cynically. "We knew that one wasn't going to fly in Congress, Lucy, but we needed to put in something we could take out. Negotiating 101."

"Yes, but it's still too bad."

"We can't boil the ocean."

It's Ms. Verita's turn to laugh cynically. "No, we can't. But when you grow up on the streets of L.A., like I did, where school walls are riddled with bullets, teachers are afraid to teach, and your representatives don't even acknowledge that you exist, you realize that you have nothing to lose *trying* to boil the ocean."

When Ms. Verita says this, I smile. I didn't know she grew up on the streets, too. She hides her roots well.

"But there's a difference between having nothing to lose, Lucy, and getting something done. Especially here in Washington." Representative Bridges sounds like someone's mom. Her advice almost seems like it's meant for me, too.

"That's why you have to move forward with this bill, Terry," Ms. Verita pleads. She's shaking her hands.

There's a brief lull in conversation. I can see Ms. Verita's shoulders slump.

"We have to decide what aspect of Democracy First is most important," Representative Bridges says at last. "For me, it's education—plain and simple. We have to get enough funding back into public education to re-create the best system in the world. There was a time when America was in the top ten, but now our public education system has even fallen behind some third-world countries. A well-educated electorate at least has a chance of cutting through the propaganda pumped at them all day long by an unethical media. It's a good starting point. I think I can whip enough of our base to support the kind of funding our public education needs. And it will make Oppenheimer's job easier in the Senate if the bill is leaner. She's already talking about tying it to a broader government funding measure so Charles can't filibuster. But if we try to force through media reform, too, Lucy, we're simply going to lose the whole bill. The media lobby is just too powerful—"

"It's hardly media reform," Ms. Verita grumbles. "We're just insisting on transparency." Ms. Verita is looking down at her laptop now. I can see her chin in the frame. It's trembling, and so is her voice when she continues. "You're right, though. Getting more funding to public schools is more important than making changes to media or campaign finance. I trust you, Terry," she says. "But whatever you do, please don't negotiate with yourself."

Representative Bridges laughs. "I don't intend to, Lucy. In fact, I intend to make Charles and his rich corporate buddies sweat a little before I strip anything out of the bill."

"Rich Supremacists," Ms. Verita mutters when she hears the phrase *rich corporate buddies.*

"I also intend to expose his bill, Real Reform, as the fraud that it is, converting public schools into work houses! Congress passed the Fair Labor Standards Act in 1938 to protect children from that kind of abuse. It's outrageous!" I hear Representative Bridges's fist pound her desk. "But we're running out of time, Lucy. We need to get this done before Thanksgiving or it will get put off to next year, which means a new Congress. And then we'll be starting all over again, or worse. We can't let Real Reform—that infernal Dummies Act—see the light of day! Charles knows that you and I are the only ones standing in his way. The vote has to happen this coming Friday or it won't happen at all."

The video ends abruptly because Ms. Verita closes her laptop. I'm guessing Julien watched this video, too, and that's how he knows Representative Bridges's game plan.

I watch some more videos, mostly those taken from Ms. Verita's webcam, but also from Oppenheimer's and Landon's staffs. The more I watch, the more I understand how valuable all of this spying is to Senator Charles. He knows exactly what the other side is planning.

My stomach begins to grumble. It occurs to me I haven't eaten in a long while, but I'm too busy digesting what I've seen to worry about my grumbling gut.

I realize that I like Representative Bridges. Even though she sounds as cynical as all the other politicians, she's trying to do what's right—at least for people like me, who have a better chance of getting struck by lightning than making it in America. Here, in Congress, the struggle between the Haves and Have Nots is being played out between Charles and Bridges.

I'm starting to understand why Ms. Verita is so worried. Friday's vote is only two days away, and it looks like all the cards are stacked against her and Representative

Bridges—and she doesn't even know what I know from Julien about Charles buying off votes in the House. And she doesn't know the extent of Julien's spying operation.

Without thinking, I send a text to Ms. Verita: Its Boot. Need 2 tlk.

I'm surprised when she texts me right back: Come by in 30. Call first.

BEAN SOUP

*T*hirty minutes gives me just enough time to sneak into the Senate kitchen and grab whatever's hot and ready. I'll call Ms. Verita from somewhere else in the building before dropping by. It's safer to move around. Not that I think I'm being traced. I got my phone from Come Up and "customized it" to work with any SIM card—standard, mini, or micro. Plus, it's unlocked so I can roam on any network.

When I got here, I had a pocketful of extra SIMs—LaQuota used to sell them hot for ninety-nine cents with no guarantee on how long they'd last. One by one, mine have been disabled by their carriers. But in here, I have access to an endless supply of SIM cards. There are lots of extra devices floating around this place. I never use the same SIM card for more than a day or two, just in case someone decides to trace it—which is unlikely. It's easier just to have the carrier disable it and issue a new one. Still, better safe than sorry, particularly now that I left my calling card in Julien's office. Things will be heating up, especially when someone thinks to check that surveillance video outside his office.

I throw on the Senate Dining Room waiter's uniform I stole, rinse and spit using a bottle of water and a travel-size mouthwash (I've lifted tons of them from staff rooms—this place really is like a hotel), and take a quick look at myself using my smartphone camera. My hair's pretty wild-looking these days, but I press it down with my hands and decide it will have to do.

As I lock my door tight, I have a sinking feeling. My days here are numbered. My run in the Capitol was going to end someday anyway, but with the Democracy First vote happening at the end of the week, and Julien doing something illegal to swing the vote, and Ms. Verita needing my help to defeat him, I get the sense that something bad is going to go down real soon.

Nothing to lose, I remind myself. And it's true. If I can help Ms. Verita take down some of these crooks before they catch up with me, at least that's something. I can't be bothered with looking past today. How does that saying go? The one my mom used as her crutch: "Yesterday is history, tomorrow's a mystery, and today is a gift. That's why it's called the present."

I never really liked that saying, because to hear it coming out of my mom's mouth it sounded like just another excuse for getting high. But it seems to fit my present circumstances (no pun intended).

I pat my pants pocket, which has the hard drive in it. I still don't know what I'm going to tell Ms. Verita, but I'm going to give this gift to her and let her figure out what to do with it.

Wednesday means bean soup in the Senate Dining Room. (Actually, bean soup has been on the menu every day for more than a hundred years. No one knows why, but there are a couple of theories about senators in the early 1900s who insisted on having it every day.)

Chicken noodle soup, Caesar salad, and Reubens are the lunch specials (minestrone soup and portobello mushrooms on focaccia if you're a vegetarian). Of course, there's a full menu in this place (think five-star hotel), so you can get just about anything you want, but the daily specials are premade and easiest to grab. The best part about it is it's free. Not just for me, but for the senators and their staff, too. Well, not exactly free. They're fond of talking about taxpayers around here—as if a taxpayer was an unwanted relative who dropped by now and then for an awkward visit. In fact, ordinary people can come eat here, but it's really expensive and hard to get reservations. Go figure.

The kitchen is adjacent to the Senate Dining Room, S-110, in the Capitol Building. There's a network of narrow service halls built when slaves worked the Capitol and had to keep out of sight as they moved around the grounds. It's those service halls that I use now to get in a kitchen side door.

As I move quickly and quietly down the old corridors, I think of the slaves who used to work here, and I can't help thinking about Ms. Verita's White Supremacists and Rich Supremacists. I know I don't know much about history, but it seems to me like she's put her finger on the dark side of America—past and present—with those two phrases.

She's really smart.

It's busy in the kitchen—Congress is in session—but since I'm in a uniform, I blend right in. At least, I'll blend in until someone recognizes that my face is not familiar. It smells so good in here that my stomach howls at me and I realize I'm ravenous. There's a row of plates ready to be loaded on a serving tray and delivered to the dining room. I'm about to grab one of the plates, which has a Reuben, soup, and salad, when one of the chefs barks at me.

"Don't just stand there, kid. Get those plates loaded. Senator Charles doesn't like to be kept waiting." The chef claps his hands in my face.

My heart skips twice. The first time because the chef called me *kid*, which, for an instant, makes me think the chef recognizes me since that's what Rhino's gang calls me. But I quickly realize there's no familiarity to the name— he's just calling me a kid because I'm so much younger than him.

My heart skips a second time at the mention of Senator Charles. It's as if the chef (or the fates) had been reading my mind. Not wanting to draw attention to myself while I think through the situation, I begin loading the plates on a tray.

"Vite, vite!" the chef urges, resorting to French and flapping his hands at me just to be a snob.

I pick up the tray and carry it shakily into the dining room. Senator Charles is easy to spot. He looks like a silver-haired vampire. His skin is bone white, his pale blue eyes practically luminescent, and even though he's old and sickly, his tall frame still lords over the table like he's holding court. His cane is leaning against the table to his right.

I've heard that it's a replica of the cane that Brooks used to beat Sumner. I wonder if it's true. That would be even more obnoxious than McElroy's gold microphone.

Julien is dining with Senator Charles and another senator—someone from Wyoming—whose name escapes me for a moment. But she's got a reputation for being a gun toter who openly carries a firearm wherever she's allowed.

I laugh to myself. These two senators, in this room, with all of the old linens and furniture, might have stepped right out of the 1850s—except that one of them is a woman.

One of the busboys sees me coming and moves a serving stand closer to Senator Charles' table. He gives me a look like, *who are you?*

I smile and shrug, but say nothing.

The busboy begins to help me serve the plates. I know right away I'm doing it wrong when Julien looks up at me and frowns.

"Where's Richard?" he says.

I shrug. "Ni idea," I say, pretending that my English is bad. I can put on an authentic Hispanic accent when I want. I learned it from my mom. "Está enfermo. Con nausea." I stick my finger in my mouth.

"But he took our order."

I shrug again. "No sé," I say, maintaining the accent and speaking slowly, as if the English words are hard for me. "Pero, don't worry. We get new plates for you when he threw up on the first ones." I grin and keep serving, but the busboy looks panicked. He suddenly stops serving and scurries toward the kitchen. My time is just about up. I'm going to have to make a hasty exit, but I can't help myself.

I have to leave my prankster calling card.

I know it's juvenile, and that Ms. Verita would be appalled, but I also think she might secretly relish it when the steaming hot bowl of navy bean soup slips out of my hand, catches the edge of the table, and douses both Senator Charles and Julien equally.

Julien leaps to his feet. "What the—" he shouts, curbing his tongue at the last minute and glaring at me.

Senator Charles can't move as fast. He pushes himself back, grabs his cane, and looks like he wants to hit me with it. Those pale blue eyes look more like daggers than irises, and the frown on his face reminds me of Scrooge.

"¡Lo siento!" I say. Just then, the head waiter rushes into the room flanked by two security guards and the busboy.

I wink at Senator Charles and Julien, laugh, and say, "¡Hasta luego!" Then I take off running, snatch a freshly served Reuben and linen napkin off of one of the tables, and race through the main door.

I can hear gasps and murmurs in the room as I exit, but I'm so focused on what's happening behind me and wrapping up the Reuben in the napkin that I crash, quite literally, into Melon who was rounding the corner.

Luckily, he's as surprised as I am, so we both end up on our butts. The difference is, he's wearing more of my Reuben than me. I spring to my feet and take off running just as the guards who were chasing me exit the dining room.

"Get that kid!" Melon bellows, scrambling to his feet.

But I'm already bounding down the stairs toward The Crypt. I dart through a group of tourists, who don't know what to think of a kid in a waiter's uniform running full-tilt through the Capitol, so they step aside for me.

I can hear the security guards in hot pursuit, but they're falling behind. Still, I'm not taking any chances after accidentally bumping into Melon. That's the second time in two days that Melon caught me by surprise. Rhino must be on high alert for me, which means I might encounter company at any moment. But I make it safely through The Crypt and into a side door that leads to the subbasement. Before heading back to my suite to change, however, I pull out my phone to call Ms. Verita. There's a text from her that's a few minutes old.

Where r u?

I text her back. On my way.

As I put the phone back in my pocket, I suddenly realize something's missing. The hard drive!

I stop short. I pat myself down in a panic. Automatically, I begin to retrace my steps, but don't find it in the service halls. I don't want to go back out into the main part of the Capitol, it's too risky. I lean against the wall and slide to the ground, swearing. It must have fallen out of my pocket when I bumped into Melon.

Now what? I can't believe it. I'm so angry with myself. If I'd resisted the temptation to mess with Julien and Senator Charles…I groan.

Ms. Verita's going to kill me.

OREO NEWS

Living on the streets, you learn to cover your tracks and keep a low profile. It's like a show I watched on Animal Planet about life in the Serengeti in Africa. All the animals live by one rule: avoid risk of injury.

Well, it's the same way on the streets.

And the streets share another thing in common with the African wilderness: predators and prey.

Most people are prey, shuffling along day after day, doing what they're programmed to do, following a routine, sticking to the rules, being good citizens.

The predators hunt the prey. Stang's a predator. My mother is prey—she's easy prey, the sickly kind, like the zebra whose days are numbered because she can no longer keep up with the herd. My dad was a predator who preyed on my mom and on others, too. In fact, he was the one who injured my mom in the first place: got her started on drugs, beat her at home, and took advantage of her. He was the mean kind of predator, the hyena who will hunt just because he has sharp teeth and big claws, and not because he's very hungry.

There are also scavengers, who follow the never-ending conflict between predators and prey and avoid all risk of injury. They let the predators do the heavy lifting, then swoop in silently to finish the job.

LaQuota's a scavenger. She lets other people do her dirty work, then she takes what's left and benefits. As scavengers go, though, she's a nice one.

I'd like to go to Africa someday, to appreciate the daily struggle up close, to see those wide-open plains filled with wildebeest and zebra, to watch a hyena snatch up a small gazelle, or catch a pride of lions taking down a massive water buffalo. That would be cool.

As for me, I don't know how I fit in to the street hierarchy. Sometimes I think I'm prey, but I'm also a predator, doing LaQuota's dirty work. But I'm good at scavenging, too. I'm stealthy, and I cover my tracks well, and I avoid risk of injury (or at least I did until I beat Stang with a baseball bat). It's why LaQuota lets me hang around her shop and pays me for the work I do. I don't attract any unwanted customers or attention.

But right now...right now I'm feeling like prey. I'm feeling like the stray wildebeest who wandered into a lion's den. I've left tracks all over this Capitol Building. I've been careless. It wouldn't be so bad if I was the only one who stood to get hurt, but I'm not. If I don't do something quick, Ms. Verita, Representative Bridges, and (if you follow that logic all the way) the American people are going to get hurt. The stakes are that high. I guess I really do have something to lose, after all (more than Ms. Verita). We all do.

I've been sitting here in the service hall, knees crunched to my chin, crying, feeling sorry for myself, not knowing what to do. I run the back of my hand across my cheeks to dry them.

Ms. Verita's waiting. I have to face her. I've heard it said that the truth will set you free. Well, I have a feeling that this time it's going to land me in jail or juvie. But I have to tell Ms. Verita the truth. Or, at least, some of it. She doesn't need to know I snuck into Julien's office, but she does need to know I lost the hard drive.

"What took you so long, Boot?" Ms. Verita asks when I slip in through her office door. "Estaba preocupada. I was starting to get worried."

I don't have the courage to look her in the eyes.

She knows something's up.

I do notice, however, that she's wearing a black-and-white striped dress that makes me think of zebras. As usual, she smells good.

"¿Qué te pasa?" She places her hand on my shoulders and steers me into one of her visitor chairs. "What's wrong? And why are you dressed in that—that waiter's uniform?"

I'm feeling so miserable, I'd forgotten all about what I was wearing. But a smirk flashes across my face as I think about Julien leaping out of his chair and Senator Charles trying to scuttle from his. My smirk vanishes as the rest of the scene plays out in my mind.

"What have you done, Boot?" Ms. Verita's tone has an edge to it.

"I have good news and bad news," I mumble.

"I always did like to save dessert for last," Ms. Verita says warily. "Let's have the bad news first."

So I tell her about my encounter with Julien and Senator Scrooge (I can tell Ms. Verita gets a kick out of my nickname for Senator Charles) in the Senate Dining Room, and my narrow escape.

"I told you to stay away from those two," Ms. Verita scolds, but there's a twinkle in her eye. I can tell she's really not mad, even though she's trying to seem so. "One of these days, Lonnigan will catch up with you and he'll show no mercy. We're going to have to get you out of here before that happens. Now, what's the good news?"

"Well, that kind of *was* the good news," I say. I'm joking, but my delivery is off.

Ms. Verita frowns. "I said I like to save the good stuff for last."

"How about an Oreo with the good news in the middle?" I say.

"Boot!" Ms. Verita plants her hands on her hips.

"Well, I was able to do some digging on that trojan."

"¿Y?" Ms. Verita is uncharacteristically impatient.

"It's worse than we thought." I don't mean to drag it out, but I'm having trouble lying to her. It's not exactly lying, but it *is* withholding the truth.

"What do you mean?" Ms. Verita leans against the edge of her desk, folds her arm across her chest, and stares at me.

I look up and meet her gaze. I swallow hard and then I tell her about the files I downloaded from Julien's server. I don't tell her how I found Julien's server, and I don't mention the trojan I loaded on his, but I do tell her what's in those files.

She looks stunned. "You mean to say he's been videotaping me?"

I nod. "Not just you, Ms. Verita, but lots of other senators and representatives, too."

"And you have these files?"

I gulp. "Well, that's kind of the other part of the bad news."

"What are you talking about, Boot?"

This is no game. Ms. Verita is furious, and doing everything to keep her cool. I don't think she's furious at me, but I can't be sure.

"Well, it fell out of my pocket when I was running out of the Senate Dining Room."

"What fell out of your pocket?" She's speaking slowly and deliberately.

"The hard drive with all of the video files. There were nearly two terabytes of them."

Ms. Verita's jaw drops. Her shoulders slump. I know I've let her down.

"But I can just log on and download another copy," I add quickly. "And I copied some of the files onto my laptop."

Ms. Verita glowers at me, but says nothing.

I start talking to fill the awkward silence. "I mean, if *you* have a hard drive, I might be able to start it right—"

"Boot, do you have any idea what this means?"

I nod.

Ms. Verita narrows her eyes as if she's assessing me. "I don't think you do, or you would not have been so cavalier with that hard drive." She pauses. I fidget. She continues.

"Have you heard of Watergate?"

I nod, but I don't really know all the details. I know it was some Washington scandal back in the 1960s or '70s, but that's about it. She can tell I don't really know.

"President Nixon had to resign his presidency because he was implicated in a wiretapping scandal. From the sounds of it, his wiretapping scandal was far less extensive than what you've discovered about Senator Charles and Julien. Your evidence, if it's true, could have far-reaching ramifications that would shake up Congress." She pauses and stares at me.

"Now, do you know where you dropped the drive?"

I nod, then shake my head.

"Which is it, Boot? ¿Sí o no?" she says coolly.

I hide my face with my hands. "I'm sorry, Ms. Verita." I haven't even told her about Julien's conversation with Lana yet. That's going to be the icing on the cake.

I hear Ms. Verita move away from her desk. Next thing I know, I feel her hands on my shoulders. It makes me jump. With the exception of squirming away from Rhino and his goons, I haven't felt someone's touch in a long time. It triggers something. Something down deep. I begin to sob. I hate myself for it, for letting her see me like this, but I can't seem to help it.

"It's OK, Boot," she says soothingly. "How could you possibly understand the significance of what's going on? I should not have asked so much of you."

"But I do understand," I say between sobs. I begin wiping away the tears. "I looked through some of the files, Ms. Verita." And then I start rambling. Ms. Verita must think I've lost my mind. "You can't go ahead with the vote this week. Senator Charles made a deal with Landon. They're going to humiliate Representative Bridges and pass their Dummies Act."

"What?" She spins me around in the chair. "How do you know this, Boot?"

It's a good thing I have a dark complexion, because Ms. Verita might have seen my face turn white. "I told you, I saw some of the files," I lie smoothly.

"You saw Landon doing a deal with Charles in one of those files?"

"Well, not like that," I say, trying to think on my feet. "But there are files of Landon and Oppenheimer and you and Representative Bridges."

"We'll get to those," Ms. Verita says. Now she's talking to me like a lawyer. "I want to know about the vote this week. How do you know about the vote? It's supposed to be a surprise maneuver."

I'm screwed. I'm going to have to tell her. But then I'm saved by the bell, literally. Ms. Verita's phone rings.

"I have to get this," she says, picking up her phone. "Yes, Terry," she says. Then she listens for a minute. "Right away."

Ms. Verita faces me. I can tell she's angry, but she's also worried, probably more worried than angry. She leans forward and places her hands on the arms of my chair, pinning me in. Her face is only inches from mine.

"Boot, listen to me. Listen to me very carefully. The people around here are very powerful and very well connected. I know you're a street fighter—I used to be one, too. So I have some faith in your ability to stay alive. But if they find out what you've done, they will think nothing of making you disappear. Do you understand me?"

I nod. Ms. Verita is scaring the crap out of me, and I didn't think that was possible in this luxury hotel.

"I have to go see Terr—I mean, Representative Bridges now. I will probably be tied up the rest of the day. But I need for you to get another copy of those files. Keep them safe and stay out of sight until I see you again. Can you do that for me?"

I nod.

"How can I get in touch with you?" she asks, standing up straight. "Should I use this number?" She points to the last text I sent her on her phone.

I shake my head and give her my legit phone number instead. But I tell her that I use other numbers all the time, so if she doesn't reach me, not to worry. I'll reach her.

Ms. Verita gives me a sidelong look while she's typing my number into her phone. Then she leans forward and kisses me on the forehead. My heart melts.

"Vaya con Dios, Boot," she says. "Now, go, and stay out of sight."

HONEYPOT

On my way back to my suite, I'm jumpy and afraid of my own shadow. It was nice to hear Ms. Verita confess that she used to be a street kid, too. But she was only doing it to put the fear of God in me.

Well, it worked. I hear Ms. Verita's words clapping the sides of my skull like an alarm bell: *They will think nothing of making you disappear.*

That's what Stang did to The Wizard. He made him disappear. At least, until The Wizard's body turned up floating in the Anacostia. I heard it was a gruesome sight. It's hard for me to believe that these suits and collars could do something like that. It's even harder for me to equate them with Stang. But now that I've watched them in action, members of Congress are a lot like gang members: sticking to their turf, taking bribes, selling votes, spying, sabotage—Democrats and Republicans, Blues and Reds, Crips and Bloods. At the moment, I'm hard-pressed to see the difference. I'll bet Ms. Verita feels the same way, growing up in L.A. and then coming to work in DC.

Luckily, I make it back to my suite without incident, but once I'm inside, I double- and triple-check my homemade locks to make sure the door can't be opened. Not that I could escape, either. If they found me here, they might not be able to get in, but they could easily lay siege to this room until I starved to death or died of thirst. The fact that this room has no escape hatch is not lost on me. I realized it from the beginning, but the hotel was already full when I checked in, so I had to take what they had available.

I flick on my laptop, rummage through my stash of snacks, crack open a warm can of Coke Zero (they only serve diet sodas around here), and strip off this stupid waiter uniform. When I'm comfortably in a T-shirt and my cargo pants, I dig through the box of electronics I've been collecting to find another hard drive. It's not a Passport, it's an eGo. It's only half a terabyte, and it's not as fast as the Passport, but it will fit most of the files. I jack it in to my laptop, make sure it's wiped clean, bring up PuTTY (which allows me to access remote servers), and log in to Julien's.

Once I'm connected, I know something's wrong. I feel my stomach flip, and not because of the stale peanut butter and cheese crackers I just wolfed down. I can't find any of the folders I'd copied before. Clearly, the server's still active since I'm logged in, but someone's been erasing or moving the files. I back out to the root directory, where I find a single MPEG file called ViewMe.

I start to click on it, but I hesitate. I know it could be

a file that drops a virus on my laptop. But I'm pretty confident that if it did, my laptop's security would pick it up pretty quick, so I decide to chance it.

The video maximizes to fill my laptop screen. It's Julien.

"This message is for the burglar who broke into my office and stole something of mine." He's sitting at his desk, using his webcam to film himself. He looks calm and he's got his Capitol Charm turned way up.

"By now, you know that what you possess is dear to me. So I have a proposition for you. An exchange, if you will. I am prepared to pay any form of currency you would like, and that includes information, scuttlebutt, and even—dare I suggest—votes, if cold, hard cash is not enough. But we must meet face-to-face to conduct our transaction." He clears his throat, presses the knot on his tie, and continues. "I am free this evening between 9:00 and 11:00 p.m. Clearly, you know where to find me. Whatever you do, do not underestimate the value of my offer. Nor should you underestimate the technical prowess of my team. This video is designed to play once, and only once, at which time it will corrupt itself irreparably. Hope to see you tonight."

As soon as the video ends, I make a copy of it onto the eGo hard drive, but as Julien promised, the file won't play, and none of the programs I have are able to open it.

I jack out of Julien's server and sit back.

I learned a lot of things working for LaQuota at Come Up. I read manuals, studied online tutorials, joined a number of hacker chats, and spent time learning how to tunnel into corporate and enterprise servers. It's how I acquired all the software we used to load up the hot equipment that LaQuota bought off the street. One of the things I learned was that big company IT shops and government agencies set up what's known as honeypots for hackers. I read a whole article about it from a guy who used to work for the CIA, but now consults to corporations for big bucks. I wonder if I could ever do that someday.

The idea behind a honeypot is to make it easy—but not too easy—to hack into a specific set of servers that are loaded with whatever the hackers might be looking for. In the case of government agencies, where espionage is the likely motive, they lace the honeypots with false information that looks official. In the case of corporate intranets, where it's mostly about theft—the article called it intellectual property—they lace their honeypots with software programs, databases, things like that. The unsuspecting hacker doesn't realize that the stuff they're stealing is traceable, either by the connection they're using or the files they're stealing.

I'm not stupid. I know that Julien has set up some kind of honeypot for me. Not the cyber kind, or my laptop would have already identified a trace program. No, he wants to lure me into his office. I hear Ms. Verita's voice again, *They will think nothing of making you disappear.* But it's to help Ms. Verita and Representative Bridges that I start to think about going to meet him. I can't stand the fact that in the video he sat there so smug, like nothing can touch him, even though I've got evidence on him that could put him away (I think).

The problem is, if he's wiped his servers clean, how will anyone know those videos were taken by him? How will they know that trojan was his creation?

Somehow, I need to get him on the record. I look at my electronics box. There's nothing in it that can be used as a discreet recording device.

I see a Windows phone lying near the top of the box. Those are the only phones that LaQuota can't sell. No one ever wants to buy a Windows phone, but right now it gives me an idea. I remember seeing something in a TechCrunch chat about a new Microsoft utility called Bing Now that uses a smartphone's microphone to record background sounds. Supposedly, Microsoft designed it to be a crowdsourcing app so people could use each other's phones to figure out where the parties are—like, which places are happening and which ones are dead. But I'm thinking I might be able to use it to record the conversation I'm going to be having with Julien.

I grab the Windows phone, boot it up, and download Bing Now from the Windows app store. I play around with it until I understand how the controls work. It's pretty cool, and it seems to have some kind of mike amplifier and audio sharpener on it—maybe that's why it works so well—because even with the phone in my cargo pocket, I can hear my voice clearly when I speak.

One of the things you learn from playing combat video games is that it's good to know something about who you're up against. Sometimes you can find a weak spot. So I decide to do a little background checking on my adversary.

Julien's not from South Carolina like Senator Charles; he's from Baton Rouge, Louisiana. It seems like he comes from a rich family—Landreau. His family name is all over everything in Baton Rouge, and supposedly there's even an old Landreau family plantation, although I can't figure out if it belonged to Julien's immediate family or to some relations. He went to Tulane for college and law degrees. Captain of the Tulane crew team. Senator Charles also went to Tulane—although many years earlier. According to an interview I found from *The Hill*, a Washington paper, the two of them met because they're both Tulane alums.

I find a few more things about some of the bills he helped Senator Charles sponsor and some of the charity work he does. I don't know much about résumés, so I couldn't tell you if his is any better than the other people around here, but he sure does seem to lead a privileged life.

I check the time. It's getting close to 9:00 p.m. In a mock gesture, I pretend to tighten an invisible tie around my neck. "Ready or not, Julien, here I come," I say. Then I unbolt my door and slip into the hallway.

I pat my pants pocket to make sure the Windows phone is in there. I may be heading into a honeypot, but at least I've got my stinger with me.

RISK OF INJURY

LaQuota always tells me I'm too cocky for my own good and that one day it's going to get me in trouble. Well, it looks like today might be that day.

I had no difficulty getting over to Julien's office. Didn't run into anyone, almost like it was meant to be. But as soon as I tap on Julien's door and walk in, I know something's up. He's sitting behind his desk, pretending to be engrossed in something on his laptop, but I can see him assessing me out of the corner of his eye.

"Well, well, so this is our little thief. The Bean Soup masquerader. I should have guessed as much." Finally, he looks away from his laptop, sits back, and knits his fingers across his chest. As usual, he's wearing a perfectly tailored charcoal suit, starched white shirt, and crimson tie. Not a hair out of place.

"You're screwed, Julien," I say. My voice is shaky, which frustrates me. I want to sound as suave and cool as he does, but I've never played this game before.

"Me?" Julien says in mock surprise. Then he chuckles, soft and low. An evil glow ignites in his eyes. Or maybe it's always there and I just notice it. Either way, I feel my stomach flip. This is about to go bad. If I was on the streets, I'd be looking around for the quickest retreat. I can run like the wind when I need to. My only exit here is the door, and if I start to back up now, I'll be signaling to Julien that I'm afraid of him. *Screw that!* I think to myself angrily. He's the crook, not me. Well, I suppose my nose isn't exactly clean, but it's not as dirty as his.

"You've been eavesdropping," I say. My voice feels stronger. "I can prove it." I hold up a thumb drive I snagged on my way out of my suite. There's nothing on it, but I didn't exactly intend to hand him my evidence. Besides, I still need to get him to confess. I hope Bing Now is doing its thing. I'll bad-mouth Microsoft for the rest of my life if it fails me.

Julien glowers at me. The word *glower* doesn't often have the chance to come up in everyday situations, but he's glowering. "On the contrary," he says at last. "You have stolen something from me that is of vital importance to national security. You are in a great deal of trouble, young man."

He's on to my game, I think to myself. It occurs to me that Julien's trying to frame me in the same way I'm trying to frame him. Suddenly, it's like a game of chess. Usually, I'm pretty good at chess (I've beat my computer plenty of times), but I haven't played on this kind of board before. He must have a recording device in here somewhere, or...

I realize my mistake too late because, just then, Melon

rushes out of Julien's closet and grabs me.

"Tie him up," Julien commands. Then he turns his attention to his laptop and begins typing as if he's just ordered a secretary to go make photocopies.

Melon is gloating. He whispers in my ear that I'm going to finally get what's coming to me as he duct tapes me into a chair. I mean, he practically mummifies me, taping my calves to the chair legs, my forearms to the chair arms, and my torso to the chair back. I can't move and it's even a little difficult to breathe, but I'm not going to give him any satisfaction by complaining.

The whole time, Julien is typing away on his keyboard. At one point, he stops to turn up the volume on the TV, but then he continues.

Finally, Melon steps back.

Julien looks up. "Thank you, Lieutenant Decker, you can go now."

For a moment, Melon looks confused. But the look on Julien's face makes it plain that Melon needs to leave, now. The oversized guard nods then backs out of the office.

As soon as Melon is gone, Julien turns into a viper. "Who do you think you are, threatening me?" he hisses. "I'm the Chief of Staff for the Majority Leader of the United States Senate, you worm!"

I shrug and give him a look like, *who cares.*

Julien gets up from his desk, walks over to me, and slaps me across the face.

That's right, slaps!

I mean, it stings and all, but I was expecting brass knuckles or a knife in the gut.

I grin at him and he slaps me again.

"Who are you?" Julien asks.

"Kid. They call me Kid," I say, stretching my lower jaw.

"Well, Kid, I want those files back, and I want your assurances that they will never surface again. Do you understand?"

"What are they worth to you?" I ask. Now the conversation is going the way I'd hoped.

Julien narrows his eyes at me. "Don't fence with me, *Kid*. Where are they?"

"Just tell me one thing," I say, trying to sound nonchalant. Here's my chance to spring my trap. "Why would you want to bug other staffers? I mean, if you're so powerful and all—*the Chief of Staff of the Majority Leader of the United States Senate*," I drawl, mockingly, "then why would you need to stoop to bugging others?"

Julien's a lawyer, and he's been working on Capitol Hill too long to walk into my trap so easily. "What is it you want, Kid?" Julien says softly, without admitting anything. I wonder if that's admission enough in a court of law. I have no idea.

"Your message to me said something about votes," I say, springing the rest of my trap. "How exactly would that work, if, for example, I wanted some votes for something like Democracy First?"

My dad was a big card player. He used to have his friends over a few nights a week. They'd sit in our little living room, under the broken chandelier, smoking cigars and drinking and gambling away the little money they had like they were tycoons. On sweltering summer nights, tempers would flare, but they'd strip down to their sweaty tank tops and keep playing, sometimes until the sun came up and they had to go to work. I learned some things about cards, watching through a crack in the wall. One thing I learned was that it's never good to overplay your hand.

Unfortunately, it's pretty clear from Julien's reaction that I've overplayed my hand. He grabs some newspaper off the coffee table, wads it up, and stuffs it in my mouth. Before I can spit it out, he's wrapping duct tape around my head. He hasn't said a word to me, which is worse than being called names. I know I'm in danger. I violated the one rule of survival: avoid risk of injury.

That's when Julien gets out the Capitol Hill equivalent of brass knuckles. He picks up the bottle of Scotch that was sitting there from his night with Lana and cracks me over the head with it. It's like an explosion of stars followed by blackness.

GET OUT OF JAIL FREE

When I come to, I'm not exactly sure that I *have* come to because it's still pitch black. But by my splitting headache, it's pretty clear that I'm awake. When I try to take a deep breath, I panic, because I'm still gagged. It takes me a while to calm down and begin breathing through my nose.

I messed up. Again! Ms. Verita could not have made it more clear to me that I needed to stay away from these guys. What do I do instead? I march right across enemy lines and into their open arms. When it comes to following instructions, I must have an IQ of zero.

Now that I've calmed down a bit and have my breathing under control, I try to wriggle my arms and legs. Nothing. Duct tape may have a million household uses, but now it has a million and one: it has to be the world's best material for tying someone up. I can't move a thing.

Now what? I need to get out of here. I try rocking the chair back and forth, thinking that it might fall over and tear the duct tape, but the closet's too tight for me to rock very far. Plus, without the ability to breathe through my mouth, I run out of breath with the slightest exertion.

Now I'm worried. No, before I was worried. Now I'm starting to panic. No one knows I'm here and I don't see how I'm going to escape. My only hope is that when Julien returns, I can talk my way out of this mess. But I have a feeling there's no talking him out of anything. He's one of those guys whose ego is as big as the moon. I crossed him the wrong way, which means he's going to want his revenge.

Still, LaQuota always says that everyone has a weakness. In Julien's case, it's probably his ego—the fact that he thinks he's so untouchable. But I can't think of a way to exploit his weakness, especially not here, sitting in the dark, taped to a chair.

I have to start thinking like Julien if I'm going to get out of this jam. What do I know about him? Not much, other than what I was able to find in his Capitol Hill profile and on the web.

I guess that if I'm Julien, I'm going to do anything to protect Senator Charles. In a way, I *am* like Julien, because I'll do anything to protect Ms. Verita. But if I'm Julien, I always want to impress the heck out of Senator Charles. I don't want him to see me make any mistakes. I don't want to risk losing my job. Maybe that's his weakness, his devotion to and fear of Senator Charles.

But before I can think of a way to exploit Julien's weakness, I hear the door to his office open and close. Right away, I can tell it's not Julien. Even though I'm stuffed in the closet where everything sounds muffled, the door was eased shut and the footfall is too light. I realize this may be my chance, so I start making all the noise I can: yelling through my gag, rocking the chair back and forth, and snapping my fingers. I tire easily, though, and stop to listen. Now there's no sound in the office.

Did I miss my chance?

Then I hear papers shuffle on Julien's desk, so a start making my muffled ruckus all over again.

Again, I stop and listen. Silence. What game is the person on the other side of the door playing? The silence lasts longer than before and I start to worry that maybe whoever it was left in a hurry. In a panic, I start making as much noise as I possibly can. The chair tilts sideways and I bang into something. I'm OK, but if someone is still in the room, they must have heard that.

Suddenly, the closet door opens and light streams in.

I'm leaning sideways, with some kind of trench coat covering part of my face, but I see right away that it's Lana.

She gasps and presses her hand to her mouth. "What's going on?" She reaches in and straightens out my chair so she can get a better look at me. "*Who* are *you*?"

I roll my eyes and arch my eyebrows as if to say, *I'd be happy to answer if I didn't have sloppy wet newspaper stuffed in my mouth and duct tape wrapped around my head.*

Lana understands my gesture right away. "Oh, oh, I'm sorry." She slides my chair out of the closet and unwraps the duct tape, pulling out a wad of my hair, which hurts like crazy. Then, with a look on her face like she's cleaning the toilet, she uses her long fingernails to tweezer out the wad of newspaper from my mouth.

I begin gulping for air. It feels so good to breathe

deeply.

"What's going on here?" Lana says. She's both angry and very worried.

"The guy who works in here kidnapped me," I say.

"Kidnapped! Why?" It's clear from her pose—hands planted firmly on her hips—that Lana doesn't believe me.

I have a snap decision to make here: how much do I reveal? If she's in on everything with Julien, and I tell her what I know, then I'm going to end up back in the closet, or worse. She might decide to call Rhino's crooked guards. I have a feeling they won't use the slapping technique to punish me. So I decide to tell Lana the truth, but only some of it. The rest I improvise. When you live on the streets and spend half your life evading the law, you learn to think on your feet.

I tell her that I'm one of the night duty office cleaners, and that I've been taking computer classes during the day to try to better myself.

"But you're so young," Lana says skeptically.

"I'm seventeen," I lie. "Dropped out of high school because it was a waste of time. Public schools suck around here, in case you hadn't noticed."

Lana turns her head and looks at me sidelong. She's still not buying it, but I can tell she's starting to come around.

"Got my GED over the summer while working nights," I lie smoothly. "But I love computers and software and gaming. Been writing code since I was thirteen."

Now she's starting to believe. "Anyway, I was cleaning this office the other day, and opened that Murphy bed closet over there to vacuum, when I noticed it was full of some really cool gear. Blade servers, solid state drives, the works."

I'm hamming it up for Lana, but I notice that her eyes are growing wide. I've struck a nerve. I can tell she knew about the servers. I have to proceed carefully.

"I was curious, so I jacked my smartphone into one of them to see what kind of OS they were running. I'm a fan of Linux—there's not enough Linux in the world, which is really too bad."

I'm rambling, I know, but Lana's shifting on her feet. She's very uncomfortable right now. As nonchalantly as possible, I nod to my hands and legs and say, "Do you mind?" meaning that I want her to unwind the duct tape. She hesitates for a second, then complies. While she's unwrapping me (there's lots of tape—Melon really did wrap me up like a mummy—so it's going to take a while), I keep talking, trying to make it sound like what happened in Julien's server closet is no big deal.

"Yeah, so, when I jacked in, I saw there were a bunch of video files. I thought to myself, *cool, this guy's got his own video server.*" I shrug. "I figure who's going to notice if I copy a few movies and take them home to watch. I mean, I'm thinking I'm going to get copies of *Django Unchained* or *12 Years a Slave* or something."

I wince. Probably should have thought of less controversial movies, but it's the first thing that popped in my head, which isn't surprising since I've had the Civil War on my mind. When I'm improvising, I find I'm not always in control of my tongue. "Or maybe *Captain America*. I like the Avengers." I'm trying to sound like a geeky teen.

"When I got home, I realized the movies weren't really

movies. They were kind of boring actually, so I deleted them. Didn't want to take up space on my phone. Videos take up a lot of space."

By now Lana's just about done undoing me. I'm helping, too, since my hands are free, unwrapping the duct tape from my right calf.

"How did you end up in Julien's closet like…that?" She points to the wads of tape lying on the ground around me.

"Well, when I came into work tonight, I knocked on the office door as usual before coming in to clean it. But the guy—what did you say his name was?"

"Julien."

"Right. Well, Julien was in his office. I started to back out and apologize for intruding, but he told me to come in. Next thing I know, he's grilling me about his servers and accusing me of stealing files."

I make my lip tremble and pretend like I'm about to cry. "I can't afford to lose this job, Miss. Honest, I didn't mean to cause harm by what I did. But he—Julien—said I was working for the Democrats or something. I've never voted in my life!" Now I'm really hamming it up. "I'm too young to vote!"

Lana pats me on the knee and nods like she's saying it's OK.

"Then he picks up a bottle of whiskey and cracks me over the head with it. Next thing I know, I'm in the closet, like you found me." I try to force some tears, but they won't cooperate. At least I've got my lips trembling and I'm able to sniffle a few times.

Lana shakes her head and pats me on the knee again.

Then she gets up and walks over to the Murphy bed closet. She opens the door and gasps, just like she did when she opened the closet door and saw me.

I come over to see what she's gasping about.

I gasp, too.

They're gone. Everything's gone. In fact, the Murphy bed is back in the closet and it's like there was never any gear in there.

"But I swear," I start to say.

Lana looks at me. We exchange knowing glances. She knew those servers were there, too. But she's not going to say so. "Just go," she whispers. "Quickly."

I turn to look at the mess we've left on the floor.

"I'll clean it up," she says. "Just get out of here. And if I were you, I'd find another job."

"Thank you, Miss," I say. I bow my head humbly. Might as well finish in character. "I know I shouldn't say so, but you're a beautiful lady."

I look up at Lana. She's blushing.

"What's your name?" she says, smiling.

"Kid. Everyone calls me Kid."

"Kid?"

"That's right." I start to rock from side to side, as if I'm embarrassed.

Lana touches my hand. "Well, Kid, I'm Lana. Now listen to me. You just got your Get Out of Jail Free card. You really do need to go, now. And you really shouldn't come back here. Ever. Do you understand?"

I nod, mumble thanks, and then back out of the door.

EXPRESS CHECKOUT

Dios mío! as my mom would say. Was I lucky! I'm practically skipping down the stairs and through the service tunnels to get back to my suite. I was sure I was going to end up like The Wizard. I knew I had a good feeling about Lana. She really is a nice lady. But it was pretty obvious she knew something about Julien's little spying operation. She expected to see servers in that Murphy bed closet, too.

But as good as I feel about having escaped, I feel equally bad about screwing things up so royally. Julien's covered his tracks well. Suddenly, I think of the Windows phone and stop short. I'd forgotten all about it. Of course, it's not in my pocket. Neither is the thumb drive I grabbed. Julien must have searched me after he knocked me out with his Scotch bottle. Good thing there was nothing on the phone or drive that could lead Julien to me or anyone else.

Julien might figure out that the Windows phone has that Bing Now app on it, but he might not know what it's for. Most people don't know squat about Windows phones and apps, unless they're geeks like me. And I'm pretty sure Julien's not the geek type. He must have someone working for him who set all that stuff up and wrote that trojan virus. In fact, I'm sure of it. His tech accomplice might figure out how Bing Now works, but it doesn't matter; there's nothing to trace back to me.

The real problem is that we've got nothing on Julien. He's going to get away with it.

Even though I know that I'm lucky to have escaped, I'm feeling miserable. About as miserable as I've ever felt in my life.

I've really let Ms. Verita down.

I have nothing for her. No way to link Julien with the evidence. All she asked me to do was get her another copy of the files I had on the hard drive and stay out of sight. I did neither. As I open the door to my suite, I realize that I can't face her. Not now. Probably not ever. That thought gets me really depressed. There's nothing left for me here. I'd have to be a fool not to see that it's time for me to check out of this hotel. Stang or no Stang, I'm in danger here, too. It seems like no matter where I turn, there's no way to avoid risk of injury.

Nothing to lose. The words sound hollow. I feel like I'm losing everything. Slipping. Look what happened to Biggie when he slipped. On the streets, you die.

I plop down on my cot and look around my room. I see my iPhone sitting next to my laptop. I reach for it, pop in my real SIM card, and turn it on, hoping that maybe Ms. Verita left me a text. After the phone boots up, I see three texts and my heart skips. When I check them out, however, my heart almost stops.

It's my mom. The first one says:

M'ijo ¿dónde estás?

Then: Boot, I need your help.

Then: Stang me va a matar.

With that last text I feel the blood drain from my face: Stang is going to kill my mom. Not only have things not cooled off since I left, but now Stang is turning up the heat.

Suddenly, it seems like everything's going wrong all at once. I have to go back to Southeast. I know I'm leaving Ms. Verita in the lurch, but I can't abandon my mom. I have to try to help her even though I know I'll be walking into an even deadlier trap than Julien set for me. So much for the code of survival.

I look around my room again, and I know it's for the last time. A tear escapes and rolls down my cheek. I wipe it away with the back of my wrist and feel the duct tape glue still stuck there. The crown of my head is sore, too, where Julien gave me that lump. Right now, I'm feeling like I deserved it.

Moving real slow, like I'm a zombie, I begin to rummage through my things, trying to figure out what to take and what to leave. I like to travel light, so I won't be taking much more than my laptop and a few mementos. But I can't leave without saying something to Ms. Verita. I grab my phone from my backpack and stare at it for a long time. I'm not going to call her—it's too late, anyway—but I should send her a text, something she'll get in the morning. Only, I don't know what to say.

Suddenly, my phone vibrates, and I'm so startled I start fumbling it like a football. It's Ms. Verita; *she* sent *me* a text! Good thing I hadn't swapped out the legit SIM card from my phone yet.

It says, R u OK?

Now I really feel horrible. It's midnight and she's checking in on me. I have to admit, it feels good that she's worried about me, but it also makes me feel worse about everything. I don't know how to reply. If I tell her what happened, it wouldn't be a text, it would be a novel, and it's not safe to send important stuff by text, anyway. One thing I've learned about using smartphones and computers is that everything—I mean everything—can be recovered, even phone calls. Face-to-face in an alley where there are no cameras is the only way to have a private conversation these days. And then you have to wonder if the other guy is wearing a wire—or recording with his smartphone. I'm too depressed to chuckle at my lame joke.

Without even thinking, I type a reply, I'm OK. C U L8r.

As soon as I send it, I know what I'm going to do. I dig through my box of electronics and find two micro SD cards—128 gigs each. That won't fit all of the video files I have on my laptop, but it will fit all of the ones taken from Ms. Verita's computer, and maybe a few more. Even if she can't pin them on Julien, she needs to see what he's been up to. So far, I'm the only one outside Julien's camp who has seen these files. For all I know, Ms. Verita doesn't believe me.

I copy as many of the files as I can, then I grab an envelope from some stationery I lifted from McElroy's desk in the Senate Chamber, and slip the SD cards in it. Then I print:

Ms· Verita

on the outside. I cross out McElroy's name in the corner, and write:

TCK

Hopefully she'll figure out that TCK stands for The Capitol Kid. Then I seal the envelope. I don't want to leave a note or anything. Too risky. Plus, I don't know what to say.

I stuff my laptop, the master access card, and a few other things in my backpack, including a snow globe with the Capitol Building inside that I swiped from a staffer's desk, look around the room one last time, and head out. It's an easy jog through the tunnels to the Cannon Building. I head upstairs to Ms. Verita's office. It's pretty late—1:00 a.m.—so I'm not too worried about running into anyone.

I knock lightly on Ms. Verita's door. When there's no answer, I use the guard's card to let myself in. I decide not to leave the envelope out in the open on Ms. Verita's desk. It seems to me that people come and go from these offices and there's no telling whose side they're on. So I tuck it to the side, halfway under a stack of papers, and figure she'll find it eventually.

I can feel myself choking up as I back away from her desk. Time to split before I start blubbering all over the room.

Rather than exit through the Cannon Building, I decide to take the long way out. By that, I mean the way I first stumbled into the Capitol grounds a couple of months ago. As I briefly explained to Ms. Verita, there's this old tunnel that runs out to the edge of the grounds to the Summerhouse. It's not really a house, more like a stone hexagonal structure with some benches for sitting and a fountain and stuff.

I read up about it when I moved into the Capitol Building. It was built by the Capitol Architect Olmsted in the nineteenth century (1879–1881, to be exact). Back then, it might have been the edge of the city in that direction. Maybe it was all trees and forest around it, I don't know. But there's a grated window that looks in on a cave of sorts—they call it a grotto—and in the grotto, where nobody can go because of the grated opening that peers in—there's an underground tunnel that runs from underneath the Summerhouse to the subbasement of the Capitol.

When I was running from Stang, I crossed the Anacostia River into Capitol Hill and found the Summerhouse by accident. I guess I was drawn to the lights around the Mall without even realizing it.

It was pouring rain that night and I needed a place to sleep that was dry. Even though the Summerhouse has no roof, the benches are sheltered. I figured I'd crash there until someone chased me away, but when I wandered in, I saw the grotto and figured that would be a great place to get out of the rain and the sight of security patrols.

I'm pretty good at scaling walls, so I climbed over and in. You have to crawl on your hands and knees for a little way, but then there's an iron hatch door with a big ring on the outside to open it. From there, roughhewn steps lead down into the tunnel...

The hatch door is heavier than I remember, but once I get my feet planted on the crumbling stone stairs, I'm able to shove it open and crawl back out of the grotto. As luck would have it, it's pouring rain again, just like the night I arrived. In fact, I get a sense of déjà vu that's so powerful, I wonder if my whole stay at the Capitol was really just a dream. But I know it wasn't. I have the snow globe in my hand that I kept shaking and staring at while I was walking along the underground tunnel.

I make sure the coast is clear, and then climb back over the Summerhouse walls. It's going to be a long walk to Come Up (it's the only place I can go), but it's OK because I need some time to think. Since it's not that cold, I don't even mind the rain. It suits my mood. I pull my smartphone from my pocket, pry open the back cover, and take out the SIM card. I throw it on the sidewalk and grind it with my shoe.

Since there's no way I'm avoiding risk of injury in the days to come, I can't have any distractions, especially not Ms. Verita, and I need to have a plan to deal with Stang, and maybe Julien, too, if I survive that long.

COME UP

It's 3:00 a.m. by the time I get to LaQuota's shop, which is near the corner of MLK and Malcom X Avenues. I know she's going to be pissed at me for waking her up, but I have no place else to go. Stang will be staking out my mom's place, but luckily that's about ten blocks south. His crew might be watching Come Up because he knows I work here—everyone does—but it's a chance I have to take. Since it's still raining and it's so late (or early), I'm thinking that I can sneak in unnoticed.

LaQuota hides a key to the back door of her building in an old tire that lies on the pavement next to a rusting car in the small fenced-in lot behind her place. The back door is the only way to get up to LaQuota's apartment on the third floor. Luckily, the key is still there in a puddle of water inside the tire.

My soggy sneakers squelch and squeak all the way up the stairs. I knock lightly on the apartment door, and after a few minutes I hear her mutter something that sounds like my name, which means she's recognized me through her peephole. A second later, I hear a chain lift, and then another (she has a couple of dead bolts, too, and a security bar) and the door opens.

LaQuota's standing there in an oversized T-shirt, holding a baseball bat in one hand and barring the door.

"Halloween's come and gone, Mr. Ghost," she says. She looks sleepy and annoyed, but I can tell she's glad to see me.

"Hi, LaQuota," I say. "Got room at the inn for a water rat?"

LaQuota looks me up and down. "Water rat? I'll say!"

I grin and start to step toward the door.

"Hold on a minute!" she says, raising her hands and pointing the bat at me. "Let me get some towels. I don't want you leaving puddles clear across the living room."

She sets the bat down and returns in a couple of minutes with an armful of towels, one of which she tosses on the floor for me to stand on.

"Who is it?" I hear Dottie call from the bedroom.

"You go on back to sleep, honey," LaQuota says. "I'll be there in a few."

LaQuota's bigger than me in every way—a couple of inches and quite a few pounds. It's hard for me to say how old she is. From my perspective, all adults seem to be about the same age unless they're really old. But if I had to guess, I'd say she was about thirty. And Dottie's probably in her mid-twenties. But I really don't know.

LaQuota takes pride in how she looks. Her hair is always done in neat cornrows and long beaded braids. She wears makeup everywhere she goes (even to bed), but it's not over the top like Dottie, who loves those long fake eyelashes and even longer fake nails. It's mostly lipstick that LaQuota likes to wear, the glossy kind that makes her lips look like they've just finished receiving a big, sloppy kiss.

"Where ya been, Boot?" LaQuota asks, once I'm stripped down to just a towel around my waist. She hands me a pair of boxers and a T-shirt, both way too big for me, which she must have grabbed while I was drying off.

"You'll never believe me even if I tell you," I say. I'm too tired to get into it. I've already got my eye on LaQuota's couch.

"Listen, honey, you get me out of bed at three in the morning, you better not hold out."

"Can it wait till morning?"

"I'm wide awake right now," she says, frowning at me. But her frown softens and finally gives way. "Fine," she concedes. "But you best not be skipping out of here before we have a chance to talk." She glares at me and I can tell that she knows about my situation already. Stang's definitely been around here looking for me.

"Scout's honor," I say with a weak grin and a Vulcan sign.

"Humph," LaQuota snorts.

"Come on back to bed," Dottie calls.

"Be right there, honey girl."

LaQuota glares at me. "Alls I have to say is it better be good, Boot."

I nod. "Thanks, LaQuota."

She snorts again and disappears back into her bedroom.

The next morning, I wake up to a clatter coming from the kitchen. With so much on my mind, I slept better than I expected. I even feel refreshed. Maybe it's just waking up to a room with the sun shining in it, something I haven't experienced for what seems like eternity.

I shuffle into the kitchen. It's clear that Dottie's not happy. She's sitting at the small, round kitchen table in a tight pair of designer jeans, and a low-cut T-shirt emblazoned with expletives, while LaQuota's frying up eggs and toast.

"Well if it isn't the midnight rambler," Dottie says sarcastically.

"That's enough, girl," LaQuota scolds. She turns to me. "Want an egg?"

I nod.

"Figures," Dottie complains. "Next thing you know, he'll be moving in with us."

"Next thing you know, I'll be smacking your bucket head with this," LaQuota says, shaking her spatula at Dottie.

"He shouldn't be here. It's too dangerous."

It's clear I walked into a domestic dispute that revolves around me.

"You know where the coffee mugs are, Boot," LaQuota says, ignoring Dottie and cracking another egg into the pan. It sizzles and smells good.

"You best save me some," Dottie warns me.

"Girl, why don't you go downstairs and get the shop ready." The way LaQuota says it, it's not a suggestion.

Dottie frowns at me, but gets up and makes her way out of the apartment. She makes sure to fill her mug of coffee on the way out.

When the door closes, LaQuota scrapes the eggs out of the pan and onto a couple of plates. She hands me a knife and points to the butter and toast that's just popped out of the toaster.

A few minutes later, we're sitting at the kitchen table together. I focus on my food and avoid eye contact, but I can feel LaQuota's eyes boring into my skull.

"Why don't you start with the part about beating Stang with a baseball bat," LaQuota says between bites.

"It's a long story," I say, looking up sheepishly from my plate.

"I got all morning, honeybun." LaQuota sits back and folds her arms as if to demonstrate the abundance of time I know she doesn't have.

If there's anyone in this world I know I can trust, it's LaQuota. I mean, she's all about making a buck and moving inventory, but she's a self-made businesswoman, which means she steers clear of the street. Well, that's not exactly true since she deals in stolen merchandise *from* the street, but she doesn't ask questions and she doesn't answer them. I know that whatever I tell her will stay with her. Plus, I don't think she wants to jeopardize the well-being of her number one employee (not including Dottie).

So I tell LaQuota about how Stang started beating me on account of my mom being so far behind on her payments, and how the next thing I knew I had a baseball bat in my hand and was dishing out more than I was getting.

LaQuota snorts in her customary way, which means she approves, but I can see the look of concern in her eyes. "You were smart to get out of here for a while, Boot. But things haven't cooled down and your mom ain't doing so good. Word is, Stang's been hanging out at your place and he's been feeding her whatever she wants in the hopes that she'll help him catch you. Doesn't take a hammer to make a grave." She points and shoots with her finger and thumb. "A person can't keep smoking the way your mom does without something giving sooner or later. Probably sooner." There's a note of sympathy in LaQuota's voice.

I grit my teeth and swallow hard. I figured as much from my mom's texts. But to hear it from LaQuota makes it more real. I feel a lump form in my throat.

My mom's a good person. She just got caught up with the wrong ones and can't seem to find her way out. Even though she hasn't been much of a mom, I can't imagine not having her around.

I nod and look down at the table. Words escape me.

"So where'd you go?" LaQuota asks. "Some said you took off for Florida or California, but I didn't believe it."

I wipe a tear from the corner of my eye, and with a shaky voice, I tell LaQuota all about the Capitol Building. I can tell that LaQuota thinks I'm lying at first, but then, as I give her more details and start to explain how things went bad there, too, I can see her eyes grow wide.

While I'm telling her everything, she gets up twice: once to make a fresh pot of coffee, and the second time to pour it. I don't really like coffee unless it has lots of milk and sugar in it, but this morning I'm drinking whatever I get.

"You're too smart for your own good, Boot," LaQuota says when I'm done. She shakes her head until her beads clack. "If it was anybody else, I wouldn't believe a word of what you just told me." She reaches out and takes my hand. "But you got potential, Boot. I seen it here in my shop, and they seen it there on Capitol Hill." She squeezes my hand. It sends a chill up my spine.

I may have potential, but right now I'm just trying to figure out how to stay alive. I've got no place to go except to find my mom, who, if what LaQuota heard is true, has a new roommate: Stang. I'm prey and the predators are closing in.

LaQuota seems to be reading my mind. "Boot, you know I'd let you crash here for as long as you like—"

"But Dottie," I say.

LaQuota scoffs and flaps her hands. "She's a bear in the morning. No, it's not Dottie that concerns me. It's Stang. If he finds out you're here, he'll burn this place to the ground trying to get to you. Come Up is all I got."

I nod. I know she's right.

"But it sounds like you made some friends over there in Oz," LaQuota says. On this side of the river, some refer to the other side, the land of monuments, as Oz. It's easy to see why—with all that white stone and marble, and dignitaries dressed up in suits and uniforms, with their helicopters and motorcades, and glamorous embassies, and ballrooms. Compared to life around here, it's like something out of a fairy tale. "There're powerful people over there, Boot. It could be your lucky break." LaQuota is referring to Ms. Verita.

I shake my head. "I told you, LaQuota, I burned that bridge."

"Not from where I sit," LaQuota says emphatically, shaking her head hard enough to clack her beads again.

"You just need to be a little more creative in your thinking. You got something going for you that those characters don't."

I give her a look like I'm not following.

"You got nothing to lose," LaQuota says.

I smile. *Nothing to lose.* Truth is, she's right. At least, sitting here on this side of the river, with a price on my head (twice on my head!), I know that LaQuota's right. I just needed a little reminder.

Suddenly, I want to go back and help Ms. Verita right away. Democracy First is being voted on tomorrow! But I need a plan. And I need to figure out how to help my mom, too. I can't leave her in Stang's hands to die.

LaQuota seems to be reading my mind again—at least the first part. She grins at me and folds her arms across her ample chest. "I'd love to mess with a senator," she says. "In a manner of speaking."

DETOUR

*T*he plan LaQuota and I come up with is a simple one, and not much different than my original plan of trying to get Julien to implicate himself.

What's different is that I'll be wired properly this time. LaQuota has all sorts of techie gear, from button cameras to high-fidelity audio recorders, wireless transmitters…you name it. It's like somebody backed up a couple of Best Buy and RadioShack trucks while I was away and unloaded them in Come Up's back room. LaQuota's been busy.

The other thing different this time is that I'll have leverage. I make a few copies of the video files and then set up an account on YouTube called DemocracyFirst. For now, it's private, but the plan is that if LaQuota doesn't hear from me by the end of the day tomorrow, she'll turn the account public and contact the press (anonymously, of course). I'm going to show Julien the YouTube videos and, hopefully, get him to freak out again, only this time I'll be wired with a real audio recorder—the kind that undercover cops use in the movies to record the bad guys. I try to use one of the button cameras LaQuota has in her collection, but no matter where I put it, it looks too obvious, and I can't afford to give away the fact that I'm going to be wired. Well, not wired. Even better: wireless. Everything that I record will be transmitting to the server in LaQuota's shop. So even if Julien finds the recorder, as long as I get him to confess before he finds it, the evidence will be safe back here in Come Up.

Since the vote is tomorrow, I have to get back to the Capitol pronto. I know that marching into Julien's office is a harebrained scheme, but LaQuota says that you don't announce when you're going to mug someone, you just do it when they least expect it. All I know is that if I have hard evidence against Senator Charles, then Representative Bridges can use that to get back the votes she needs.

The way LaQuota put it was to "blackmail the black-mailers."

At a minimum, Representative Bridges can use the evidence to stop *any* bills from being voted on tomorrow, including The Dummies Act. That way nothing will get passed, which at least buys more time.

But before I head back to Oz, my plan is to cruise through my neighborhood—I have to see for myself what's going on, see if Stang really is hanging around our place. I know that if I want to help Ms. Verita, I can't risk going after my mom right now, but I'm really worried about her.

LaQuota tells Dottie to help get me ready for my return trip while taking turns at the counter downstairs. Complaining all the way, Dottie washes my clothes for me during her breaks from the shop, and LaQuota helps me get everything else together. To my surprise, Dottie lends me a navy blue thermal hoodie because the forecast is for cold weather. "But you best bring that back to me in mint condition, Boot," Dottie warns. "Or you'll be owing me two of them!"

By late afternoon, I'm ready to go. It's been leaked in the news that the Speaker of the House, Landon, intends to bring Democracy First to the floor for a vote tomorrow, before the Thanksgiving break (LaQuota looked it up, mostly because I think she needed some evidence to corroborate my story). I'm sure that one of Julien's staff leaked it to spook Representative Bridges and her staff. Now that the cat is out of the bag on Capitol Hill about the timing of the vote, I'll bet Ms. Verita *is* panicking. She's probably worried about me, too. I feel horrible, but I'm going to try to fix it.

LaQuota gives me an extra-long squeeze before I split from her apartment. "You be careful, Boot," she says softly. "I have high hopes for you."

"Thanks, LaQuota. And you, too, Dottie." I nod to Dottie, who's lingering just out of sight in the kitchen. I hear Dottie snort the way LaQuota does. It makes me laugh.

But I have a bad feeling as I descend the back stairs. I haven't told LaQuota about the detour I'm planning to take to my neighborhood. Everything in my brain is screaming at me to head straight to the Capitol—that going back to the nabe is a really bad idea—but something tells me that if I don't see my mom tonight, even just through a window, I might never see her again. Call it street instinct.

I can't think about it. I just have to do it. She's my mom. But I can't jeopardize my mission for Ms. Verita, either. I'm just going to have to think like a predator...and get lucky. *Really lucky.*

By the time I scale the fence behind Come Up (it's too risky to take the sidewalk until I'm a few blocks away), the sun is setting and streetlights (the ones that work) are winking on. It will be easier for me to sneak up to my mom's row-house apartment in the dark. Since it's a bit of a walk from here, it will be plenty dark by the time I get there.

I pull my smartphone from my pocket and send a quick text to Ms. Verita: It's Boot. Can we talk L8r?

It doesn't take long for Ms. Verita to reply, but I don't understand her text. It says: <403>. That's it. I'm thinking maybe it's a network message, like her phone's been disconnected or something. Not good. I know Ms. Verita would not have changed her number, and I'm sure she pays her bills. If she's mad at me, she might be blocking my texts and calls, but I know she won't recognize my number because I'm using a new SIM card and a different number. As far as I know, there's no way to block texts from unknown numbers. Spammers and hackers know that, which is why they always get through.

I don't have time to text Ms. Verita again, because I need to keep my eyes on the street, but now I'm even more concerned. Maybe something happened to Ms. Verita. Maybe that's why her phone's out of service—if that's even what 403 means.

I decide to walk down Brothers Place and then keep to

the edge of the trees along the Anacostia Freeway rather than marching straight down MLK or 4th Street, which would be the same as waving a banner that I'm back in the nabe.

I feel safer with the trees on my right. If I need to, I can disappear into them and then make my way back up the river to the Frederick Douglass Memorial Bridge.

By the time I get to Atlantic Street, I'm going to have to chance the sidewalk. But I decide not to stay on Atlantic because it cuts through the heart of Stang's territory. His crew cruise up and down Atlantic all day and night in their war wagons. Instead I head down to Chesapeake Street, and cut over from South Capitol onto Brandywine, and from there to 1st Street. I decide to cut across the Oxon Run River (it's more of a brook)—that way I can stay off the streets longer.

My mom and I live on 4th Street, near Atlantic.

I'm out on the sidewalk now, and my heart's pounding against my rib cage like an angry prisoner in his cell.

Suddenly, I hear a familiar turbo muffler. Before I have a chance to duck out of sight, a navy blue Mazda with tinted windows pulls up.

"¡Mira!" someone shouts from the car window. The tires chirp as it comes to a sudden stop.

"Boot! What are you doing here?"

I thrust my hands deep into my pockets and walk up to the window. "Ant-Man. ¿Qué lo qué, amigo?"

"Yo, dude, you got some cojones showing your face. I thought you'd be in California by now. That's what I been telling everyone."

"Thanks, man," I say. And I mean it.

Ant-Man opens the car door. "Get in, amigo, before anyone else sees you."

I climb into his car. Even though I'm only thirteen (going on fourteen), me and Ant-Man are in the same grade—that is, when we go to school. He's seventeen, but he's been left back twice, and I skipped a grade, so that's why we're both freshmen at Ballou STAY High School. And it's also why he has a car and a driver's license.

"S'up, Boot," Blue says. He's sitting shotgun. Ant-Man is like Blue's private limo driver. Since Blue doesn't have wheels, he gives Ant-Man gas money to drive him around.

"Hey, Blue," I say as I fold myself into the backseat.

As soon as I'm in, Ant-Man jumps back in the driver's seat and takes off. "So, where ya been, bro?" he says, studying me through his rearview mirror.

"Hiding out." Before Ant-Man can start asking me a thousand questions, I start talking, using his real name so he knows I'm serious. "Hey, Antonio, you think you can drop me off around the corner from my mom's?"

"¿Estás loco? I wouldn't be going there!" Ant-Man says. A worried look clouds his perma-grin face. "Stang's been hanging out there with his crew."

"I got to see my mom," I say, sounding more desperate than I want. It almost comes out like I'm a whiny little kid.

Ant-Man shakes his head. Blue's not happy with my request, either.

After braking for a few more stop signs, Ant-Man says, "I can take you to the Terrace."

He means Livingston Terrace (not Atlantic), which is a couple of blocks away from my mom's place. "Cool. But can you cruise by her place first so I can see what I'm up against?"

"Only if you keep out of sight in the backseat," Ant-Man says. "I don't want trouble with Stang."

"Ten-four."

When he turns onto Atlantic, I slink down in the back. Not that anyone can see me anyway through his tinted windows, but I get why he's so nervous. No one crosses Stang without paying for it.

Ant-Man starts narrating as he turns onto 4th Street. His voice is shaky. "Pana, you can't go in there. Stang's got a car out front and a couple of war wagons. And I see at least two of his boys hanging around the street." He eyes me through his rearview mirror. "It's been like that since you left, Boot. Stang's been all over your mom..." He bites his tongue too late. "Sorry, dude, I didn't mean nothin'—"

"It's alright," I say.

I sneak a peek through the window. It's Stang's rust-colored Mustang, with custom rims (Asantis with chrome hundred-dollar bills and Gorilla hub covers) and blue LED lights under the runners, that's parked out front.

No one says anything for a couple of blocks. Finally, Ant-Man pulls over.

"Don't do it, Boot," he says, getting out of his car so I can climb out of the backseat.

"I'll be alright, Ant-Man." I reach out my hand for a pound.

"That's the problem—no, you won't." Ant-Man grabs my hand and pulls me to him. He claps me on the back. "You're the smartest bro I know," he says in my ear, "but you're acting dumb right now. Why are you being so stubborn? ¿Por qué?"

It's not a question he expects me to answer. More loudly, for Blue's sake, he adds, "Be cool."

"Gracias, amigo." I turn away from Ant-Man and head up the street. Dogs start barking as soon as Ant-Man floors it and roars away.

I figure the best way to get a glimpse into my mom's place is from the roof next door. My guess is the roof won't be guarded. If I'm lucky, I might be able to see her through the back windows. I'm just hoping my mom's alone when I get there, which is unlikely if Stang's car is out front and his crew is watching the street. But he has his crew drive him all over, so it doesn't mean that he's in there for sure. And since our apartment is on the top floor, I only have to go down one flight of stairs if I decide to go in, *which*, I tell myself, *I won't.*

Beyond the roof, I don't really have a plan. I'm just thinking that if I see my mom then something good will happen.

You know you have a bad plan when 100 percent of it is based on hope, and I know I'm breaking every rule of survival on the streets or in the wild, but I have to see my mom before I head back to the Capitol. I just have this bad feeling that we won't be seeing each other for a long time. If she doesn't die, which is what worries me most, I might land myself in jail or juvie going after Julien.

Maybe I should be more afraid of Stang than I am, but, in truth, it's Julien that scares me more. It's because I know what Stang will do to me, but Julien's unpredictable. Well, not entirely unpredictable since I know he has no problem with kidnapping me, taping me up, and stuffing me in his closet, but I have a feeling that the next time our paths cross, he won't be so lenient.

All of the row houses on this block are three stories tall and connected. Because the street is on a hill, there're a few feet from one rooftop to the next, but at least there's no alley to hurdle.

There is, however, an alley in the back, and all of the buildings have little courtyards. Some are paved, some have a little plot of grass. Ours is the only one with a tree, but it's pretty dead looking, even for this time of year.

I hear more dogs barking farther up the alley as I climb one of the fences. I'm just tall enough to make the leap to the ladder hanging from the bottom of the fire escape stairs. I need to get to the roof without anyone spotting me, which is hard to do on a metal staircase that creaks and groans, but I'm lucky, because all the lights are dark in the building I pick.

I pull myself up on the roof and press myself flat against it. I lie there for a few minutes just to make sure that no one followed or spotted me. When I'm sure it's cool, I get up and begin moving hunched over up the street. It's easy to climb from one rooftop to the next. The trick is to do it quietly so that the people living on the top floor don't hear you and come up to investigate or call the cops.

I get to my mom's roof and realize the first flaw in my plan: there's no way to see inside her place without climbing down the fire escape. It's so old and creaky, you might as well ring the front doorbell. Right then and there, I make a snap decision to try to get into our apartment. I think I knew all along that I would try to get in because what I really want is to hug my mom and tell her it will be OK. Actually, what I really want is for *her* to tell *me* that everything will be OK, but I know that's not going to happen.

I take a moment to rest by the door that leads down into the building. From here, I have a clear view of the Capitol Building and Washington Monument, which are lit up like jewels. They seem so close to me, maybe a couple of miles, and yet there aren't enough miles in the universe to measure the distance between the world beneath my feet right now and the world over there. Life here is so raw, so desperate; nothing comes easy. Life over there is so cushioned, so calculated; *everything* comes easy—although they pretend not to know it.

The moon is setting toward the Monument, which gives it a mystical aura. Like something out of ancient Egypt—some kind of lightning rod to the gods. And a cold wind keeps gusting off the river. It's a north wind, judging by the direction, and I can see clouds moving in, getting ready to swallow the moon. Looks like rain—or maybe even snow.

I shiver.

No more stalling.

I ease the door open and tiptoe down the stairs.

THE WRATH OF STANG

I guess Ant-Man was right to call me dumb and stubborn, but sometimes you have to go with your gut. Stang knows my mom's a junkie, and he knows the best way to kill a junkie and get away with it is to give them what they want.

I creep down the stairs from the roof and crouch at the last step to get a good look down the hall. It's dark. The lightbulbs in these halls never last long. Someone always smashes them. Dark is the criminal's friend. But right now, it's my friend, too.

As usual, the hall reeks like urine and puke and who knows what. All of the apartments in here are rented by junkies, and Stang's the one who supplies them all. Same goes for a bunch of the buildings around here. I feel bad for the respectable people who live in the area and are just too poor to move, especially the old ones like Mrs. Smith. She takes me in sometimes because she knows I'm not a junkie like my mom. I help her out, too, by doing her grocery shopping and helping her with her TV—I tapped into Comcast's cable for her so she could watch a few channels. In fact, LaQuota let me bring her a new TV last year, for free. Mrs. Smith acted like it was Christmas, baking me cookies to take to LaQuota and Dottie. But she was the exception. It's never any good when a drug dealer takes over your neighborhood. Especially a heartless killer like Stang.

Fortunately, no one's guarding the door to my mom's place. Moving as fast and light as I can, I dart down the hall and stop at the door to listen. I don't hear anything other than the TV, which is on low. That's good, too. If Stang was in there with some of his crew, they'd be jawing every couple of minutes. At least that's what I convince myself as I ease the door open.

The place is a filthy wreck. Worse than I imagined. It stinks like rotting food and that sweet, cloying smell of narcotics being cooked all day long. I have to hold my breath to avoid gagging.

The layout of the apartment is simple. Tiny matchbox kitchen to the left. Short hall. Living room on the left. A bathroom after that, and a bedroom at the end of the short hall.

I take the few steps toward the living room, expecting someone to step out. My heart is hammering again. I feel like I'm in one of those thriller cop movies where the bad guys are about to jump out, guns blazing. But when I peek into the living room, I see my mom, just sitting quietly on the couch. A thin halo of sweet-smelling smoke swirls above her head. Her face is sunken, like she's some kind of ghoul or zombie, and the hue of her skin is blue, mostly from the TV, but I have a feeling it wouldn't look much different even in the light of day.

I step into the room. At first she doesn't see me. Then her eyes focus and a puzzled look crosses her face. Her eyes focus some more, and then they grow wide. She drops the pipe in her lap and claps her hand to her mouth. Before she can form words, tears come to her eyes. She tries to stand up, but it's a pretty feeble effort.

"¡Dios mío!" she finally says in a hoarse voice that sounds like she's fried her vocal chords. "Henry!"

I step toward her and kneel down by her side, taking her hand. She leans forward to hug me.

"Mom, you've got to get out of here."

"Oh, Boot!" she says more loudly, and she begins to sob. Her frail body shakes as I pull her toward me.

Suddenly, she pushes away. "No!" she says. She looks alarmed. More than alarmed. Wild-eyed and afraid. "You have to go, Boot," she hisses. "¡Ahora mismo!"

"I'm not going anywhere without you, Mom!" I say, sounding more resolute than I feel. This wasn't the plan. But seeing her, there's no way I can leave her here. "We need to get you some help."

"That's right," says a cold voice behind me. "You won't be going anywhere."

I spin around in time for Stang to thump me hard above my eye with the butt of his gun. I fall back into the coffee table and scramble out of the reach of a second blow. I can feel blood trickling into my eye.

My mom lets out a hoarse cry. "No, Stang! I'll do anything. Just let him go. Por favor—"

"Shut your mouth," Stang hisses. "I'll deal with you

later."

My mom's too weak and confused to put up much of a fight, but she stumbles off of the couch, only to be hurled by Stang into the hall, where she crashes into the wall and falls in a heap to the floor.

I use the distraction to leap to my feet, but Stang has his gun pointed at me. Stang's skin is extra dark, like he got left in the oven too long, or, in his case, like he crawled out of the fires of hell. His teeth flash in the dim light, and he's strong, naturally built like the lion that's born to lead a pride.

"I see you got my texts," Stang says, holding up my mom's phone. He smiles deviously. "Don't worry, Boot, I don't intend to kill you right away. I plan to make an example out of you, like I did The Wizard. I hear people been saying I've been going soft, letting you get away. Well, we'll see who's slipping."

Stang lunges at me. He's taller than me and probably twice my weight. I can't do much to defend myself, especially in such close quarters, but I drop to my knees and steamroll toward him. He trips, and I use the opportunity to leap toward the hall. I take two quick steps into the hall, turning toward the bedroom, away from where my mom's lying unconscious, but Stang's on me. He tackles me to the ground and begins beating me with the butt of his gun. Each time he hits me in the head, I see stars, but somehow I'm still squirming toward the bedroom.

Stang's got his knee drilled into my back, but I'm mostly protected by my small, makeshift backpack, which is hidden under the hoodie and has my laptop in it and a few other goodies from LaQuota's shop. Just when I think

I can't take another blow, I hear my mom screech. She hits Stang over the head with a bottle, which shatters all around us.

Stang falls back, which is all I need to get to my feet. I don't even think twice about what I do next.

In one big leap, I crash right through the bedroom window, which is three stories up. But it's not like the movies, where the glass shatters neatly and the hero lands on his feet at a full run.

The impact knocks the wind out of me and the glass turns into lethal blades. But my biggest concern is that I'm twenty-five feet in the air when the window explodes out of its frame.

I begin flailing my arms toward the dying courtyard tree. Somehow, I'm able to ricochet off a couple of the branches, which slows my fall. I expect to break both my ankles when I land, but in case you couldn't tell, this is my *lucky* day. I land in a heap of garbage. I mean a *big* heap.

As soon as I land, I hear gunshots and little smacking sounds hitting the plastic and debris around me. I roll out of the garbage pile and stumble toward the back fence. Somehow, I still have the strength to pull myself over the top and drop down to the other side. Stang hasn't stopped firing his gun, but I don't think I've been hit.

By now, dogs are barking like crazy and I hear shouts heading in my direction.

I know I don't have much time. I stagger across the narrow alley, duck between two houses, and stumble out onto 3rd Street. Unbelievably (like I said, it's my *lucky* day), I happen to stumble out just as a metro bus is pulling into its stop almost right in front of me.

As soon as the bus door opens, I lunge toward it and stagger up the steps. The bus driver looks at me and says, "No way! You get off my bus."

"Please," I beg him. "Just one stop. I'll get off at the next stop." He's about to say no when we hear more gunshots and a couple of Stang's crew come running down the street. In an act of self-defense, the bus driver slams the door shut and floors it, running right through the red light on Atlantic Street.

I fall to my knees and hold on to the nearest seat.

He keeps roaring down the road, blowing past one stop after another until he feels like he's put enough distance between him and trouble.

The passengers in the back don't seem to mind missing their stops. When I first got on the bus, I could hear a few comments supporting the bus driver's stand against me, but as soon as he took off, they all went quiet.

Finally, at the corner of MLK and 4th, he stops the bus and says, "Now, get out."

I've left blood on his floor and seats, and I can only see him with one eye, but I tell him thanks and stagger out into the street.

CODE BREAKING

*R*ain is good for washing things away. It's also good for obscurity. People tend to get distracted by rain—even a light rain like what has just started falling from the dark and dreary sky—so they don't get a good look at who's moving past them on the street.

When I start weaving up MLK Avenue, I'm certain that I'm going to get picked up—if not by DC Metro brass, then by Stang's crew. I'm a mess, and I know it. I'm swaying back and forth like I'm wasted, my head is throbbing, I can only see out of one eye, and I can feel blood crusted to my face. I have a big gash in my forearm that won't stop dripping blood (Dottie's going to kill me when she sees her sweatshirt) and my pants are torn at the knees. Plus, I'm crying.

Crying openly.

Not because of my injuries, although that would be reason enough. I'm crying for my mother. She looked all but dead. My poor mom. She's a kind and gentle soul, but she's sick and there's no help for her. And that's the worst feeling of all. I remember her telling me, "When you give up, mijito, you give in." What she meant was that if you give up hope, you give in to drugs and crime.

But I'm out of hope, Mom! I can't help you, not without getting killed myself, and what help would that be?

It's a horrible feeling, watching your mom waste away—and not because of cancer or anything, but because she lived in a place without opportunity, where she eventually lost hope and gave in to drugs.

I try to use the heels of my hands to stop my tears, maybe push them back into my face. I don't want to cry because I'm angry, too. Angry that she did this to me. Angry that all she's ever thought of is herself. Part of me knows that's not really true, but having barely escaped our apartment, I feel that way now.

I must be some spectacle—weeping and muttering, and all banged up like some crazy homeless person, like Joey Jacks or Missy Marbles (no one knows their real names), who live under the South Capitol Street overpass. I'm tempted to pull up the hood on my hoodie, but that'll attract attention more than the tears and cuts and bruises. A street kid hiding inside his hoodie…they shouldn't even bother selling hoodies to kids like me.

I try getting into a bathroom at the Valero to assess the damage and clean myself up, but the gas attendant chases me away. I need to keep moving up MLK to get to the South Capitol Street Bridge. The sooner I'm on the other side of the river, the better my chances of surviving the night.

I see a patrol car up ahead, cruising real slow, which means trouble. But just as I brace myself to get stopped, the skies really open up and it starts to pour.

Did I mention it was my *lucky* day?

It's a cold, hard rain that sends most pedestrians running for cover and makes it less likely for anyone to spot me or pick me up. I pull the hood up on my hoodie, which doesn't look so suspicious now that it's pouring. The patrol car brakes for a minute as it's passing me, but I keep my chin to my chest and do my best to walk a straight line down the sidewalk. The cops move on. If it hadn't started pouring, they would have at least rolled down their window to question me and that wouldn't have gone well.

The rain feels good. I raise my head to it and use it like a shower to wash away the blood. My forearm's still dripping, but I take one of the strings off my backpack and tie it just above my elbow. That seems to help. I tuck my backpack under the front of my T-shirt and sweatshirt with my arms wrapped around it to try to keep the electronics dry, and pick up my pace. I'm still hurting, but, man, the rain feels good. And at first, the cold air that came in with the rain feels good, too. Like applying ice to all my lumps and bruises. But by the time I get to the river, I'm shivering. That cold front came down on DC like a freight train, bringing with it the first taste of winter.

As I cross over the Frederick Douglass Memorial Bridge (aka South Capitol Street Bridge), a few snowflakes begin to mix with the rain, which makes it seem less wet, but even colder. Soon my problem is frostbite. I'm so cold that any lingering wooziness is gone and I'm not staggering anymore.

I can see the Capitol Building dome from here.

To take my mind off of my open wounds and frozen digits, I begin reciting random facts about the building, like: the dome is made of nearly nine million pounds of cast iron, and, ironically, the Statue of Freedom on top of the dome was built and raised by slaves. It's a statue of a lady who wears a crested helmet of war rather than the simple knit cap of a freed slave (the knit cap tradition comes from Roman times). A war helmet is a strange headdress for a statue of freedom, but it's probably because the irony of slaves erecting a statue of freedom was not lost on the architect of the statue, Thomas Crawford, so he decided to steer clear of the controversial knit cap. I keep running through these facts that I've memorized, but, of course, my mind migrates to the more violent bits of trivia, like, for example, that in 1890 a former Kentucky congressman, William P. Taulbee, was shot and killed inside the Capitol Building by a reporter, Charles Kincaid, on the stairs leading down to the House dining room. Kincaid claimed self-defense and was acquitted by a jury.

By the time I get to the Summerhouse on the edge of the Capitol Building grounds, my teeth are chattering and I'm so cold I can barely focus on the trivia. But the rain has stopped and only a few lazy snowflakes wander through the air, prolonging their lives by staying off the ground where they will inevitably disappear into dark pools and puddles.

I scale the brick walls that enclose the Summerhouse grotto and find the hatch that leads to the secret tunnel, but my fingers are too cold and I'm shaking too hard to get a good grip on the iron ring and pull it open. For a few minutes, I sit with my back to the cave wall, my knees

Capitol Kid

drawn up to my chin, before trying again. Eventually, I'm able to get in and I feel instant relief. The tunnel is still warm and dry—at least relative to outside.

I shuffle down the tunnel toward the Capitol Building. When I feel like I'm about halfway there, I decide to stop and gather myself. I pull out my phone and check the time. It's 8:00 p.m. I've got to get in to see Julien, but there's not much time.

I'm trying to switch gears from my mom and Stang to what I have to do next, but my emotions get the better of me. I start crying again, uncontrollably. I'm glad no one's around to see me. After a few minutes, I feel the tidal wave pass and I know I'll be able to switch gears, because I begin thinking of Ms. Verita. I know she needs me to be at my best.

I check the wires under my shirt to see if they're still working. Miraculously, they are. I don't know how they stayed intact when I crashed through that window and bounced off the tree, but LaQuota did a nice job taping them to my ribs. Did I mention how useful duct tape can be?

I use my smartphone camera to examine my injuries— the ones I didn't avoid. My face looks like a prize fighter's after fifteen rounds in the ring. How am I ever going to sneak past security to get to Julien's office?

I decide to text Ms. Verita again. I keep it simple: It's me, Boot.

I get a response pretty quick: <100>.

What the heck is going on? I send her another text: ??

Again, I get a quick response, and again it's some cryptic code: <101>.

Now I'm wondering if maybe Julien figured out a way to intercept Ms. Verita's texts since he lost access to her laptop. After all, the big vote is tomorrow and he won't want Senator Charles flying blind. I'm pretty sure they didn't hack one of the big cell networks—it's possible, but that's, like, CIA-level hacking. It's really hard to do, plus they'd be in a heap of trouble if they got caught. More likely, they hacked Ms. Verita's phone, which is easy, but would they have done such a bad job with the hack that her phone is sending out random error codes? I doubt it. Whoever is working with Julien on the tech side knows what he's doing. Screwing up a virus so bad that a phone sends error messages whenever someone texts the device it's infiltrated is the quickest way to get found out. Something else is wrong.

I'm worried about Ms. Verita. I start to imagine all sorts of dastardly ways that Julien might have gotten to her.

I pull out my laptop, which has some condensation on it, but otherwise survived the downpour. It boots up fine, and in no time, I'm trying to log in to the Capitol VPN. I figure if I can get into the control center, I can start looking at surveillance cameras to see what's going on.

But the Wi-Fi signal down here is too weak, so I pack up my laptop and move on. I decide to move closer to the guard station—to where the old service tunnel runs beneath the Senate subway. When I get there, I can hear the whir of the subway running back and forth, which means it's busy in the Capitol tonight.

I pull out my laptop and try logging in to the Capitol VPN again. The Wi-Fi signal is strong, but my ID/password combination keeps getting rejected. That can only mean one thing: they're on to me. While I was gone, Julien must have started covering his tracks. I'm guessing he had his tech guy purge some of the system administrator tables—that's where user IDs get stored.

But I was able to hack my way in through the Capitol Building's VPN once before, so I type in the home web page address. But I must have fat-fingered a key because instead of getting the secure intranet home page, I get a 404 error—page not found.

And then I feel lightning strike—not the life-changing kind that people talk about—but it's still the good kind of lightning. I hear Ms. Verita's voice telling me (somewhat defensively): *I took a Web Design and Coding class in college. I can hold my own with HTML and CSS.*

Web Design and Coding—404—Ms. Verita's texts. I can see these three facts standing side by side, like they were all shaking hands with each other.

With a small rush of excitement, I look up the HTTP codes. Those are the codes websites use to talk to each other. 404 means page not found. 100 means continue or proceed, 101 means to switch protocols. I scroll back through my texts. When I texted Ms. Verita that it was me, Boot, she sent me a 100, which means proceed. She wants me to say more, but she doesn't want anyone to know she knows who she's conversing with. Either someone's looking over her shoulder or she suspects her phone is compromised.

The next text I sent her was two question marks, and she sent me a 101. She wants me to switch protocols. I feel another small rush of excitement. I think I figured out what's going on! Ms. Verita wants me to use HTTP codes to communicate. It's pretty weird, but it's also really smart. No one will ever know what we're saying.

I feel a small sense of pride. I guess she had confidence I would eventually figure it out.

I send Ms. Verita a fresh text: <101>.

Instantly, I get a <100!> back. That's with the exclamation point, which tells me I'm right.

I don't know HTTP codes by heart, so I stare at the list on my laptop to memorize them. After a minute, I think I've got them down.

I send her a <200>, which means OK; like, I'm OK.

Then I send her a <359-CHOB>. It's not an HTTP code, it's her office number in Cannon, but it seems cryptic enough.

The next text from Ms. Verita says <403!>. Again with an exclamation point. It means forbidden. She's telling me not to go near her office. I really wish I had access to the Capitol's Security Control Center right now so I could check video surveillance. I'm flying blind here.

Suddenly, I get hit by another mini-bolt from above.

I smile to myself. It must be the first time I've smiled since I escaped from Stang, because my face hurts all over. I still have Rhino's ID, which was how I hacked my way in before and set up my own account.

My luck seems to be holding out because, as expected, Rhino's too dumb or lazy to change his password even when security is clearly doing a sweep of their computer systems and he's the head of security.

While I'm logging in to check video surveillance, Ms. Verita sends me another text: <307> followed by <H-107>.

307 means redirect, but 107 or H-107 doesn't exist.

I'm stumped for a minute when I realize that she's telling me to go to H-107 instead of her office. I'm pretty sure I know that H-107 belongs to the Majority Leader of the House—Representative Bridges.

Why would Ms. Verita want me to go to Representative Bridges's offices? (H-107 is more than one office; it has a suite, conference rooms, and balcony—I've visited it before on one of my midnight raids). Then it occurs to me. The big vote is tomorrow. Everyone must be camped out in her office preparing for it. That explains why I hear the subway overhead running back and forth nonstop between the Senate administrative offices and the Capitol Building.

I send Ms. Verita a <202>, which means acknowledged.

She sends me back a ☺, which makes my heart melt. I was afraid she was pissed at me, but now I know she's concerned and wants to see me. But I still have the matter of Julien to deal with. I really need to get that evidence.

"Let's see if I can find the snakes in the grass," I mutter to myself as I bring up the video surveillance system using Rhino's ID. As I suspected, Representative Bridges's office is a hive of activity. I switch from camera to camera, searching the conference rooms for Ms. Verita. Then I catch a glimpse of her in Representative Bridges's main office along with the Chief of Staff and a few others. Must be a strategy session.

I check in on S-106. That's an office I know by heart. It's the grandest of the Capitol Building offices and it belongs to the Majority Leader of the Senate, Senator Charles. It, too, has a complex of rooms, but all of these are as opulent as a French palace, more luxurious than anything on the House side of the building. It's just as busy as Representative Bridges's offices.

I smile cynically. It's like watching a movie with two opposing generals, preparing their battle plans, marshaling their troops, readying for war. And yet there's something very discouraging about this image because they're both Americans—we all are. You wouldn't know it, though, because our national leaders, and their followers, make it clear that they're at war with one another every day. They even use terms like "*War on this*" and "*War on that*." I mean, I know they make movies and TV shows of politics—*West Wing* and all—but I have to believe that what goes on in the White House is easy street compared to Congress. Then again, I'm just a thirteen-year-old kid.

I spot Julien at the head of one of the conference tables in the S-106 suite.

My heart sinks. How am I supposed to get to Julien in *that* hornets' nest? I don't have any good ideas at the moment, but I don't linger on that problem because I want to know what Rhino and his gang are up to. Plus, I don't want to spend too much time surfing around on his ID. If they've heightened security, they'll probably be tracking session times and login locations, which would make this particular session stand out.

When I bring up the guards' command center, I have to laugh again. They're in there eating cupcakes—literally—and one of them has a lit candle in it. Chase is wearing the party hat, which means it must be her birthday. Loki is sneaking a second cupcake, and Melon is licking his fingers. Rhino's nowhere in sight. I'd feel better if I knew where Rhino was—it's unlike him to skip dessert—but I decide the best thing to do is log off.

Seeing my familiar haunting grounds again boosts my confidence. When I formed my plan with LaQuota, I decided it wasn't safe to go back to my suite. But now, seeing those goofball guards again (who pale in comparison to Stang), I decide to take the chance. I need to change my shirt and clean up a little.

I'm smiling on the inside (my face hurts too much to smile on the outside) as I pack up my laptop and head out. With all their preparations and calculations and strategies, the two warring generals camped out on opposite wings of this esteemed and historic building aren't accounting for one small detail: me.

PRISONER OF WAR

It feels good to be home, but it's not exactly a homecoming. I mean, I was only gone, what, twenty-four hours? Less. It's not like everything's covered in dust and cobwebs. But it feels like maybe it should be—so much has happened since I left.

More than anything, what makes my suite feel different is my mom. I know I can't stay here this time. I'm just passing through to help Ms. Verita bag Julien, and then I'm gone. I need to get back to my mom before it's too late. Stang's going to kill her. He doesn't need to use bullets. I could tell she's got one foot in the grave already. That hollow look on her face haunts me. I feel like crying when I think of it, but I'm also angry. I'm tired of being Stang's prey. I want to be the predator.

Maybe the comfort of my suite is giving me too much confidence, but somehow I'll find a way to take on Stang and save my mom. Right now, I don't care if I die trying.

I know I felt different about that a few hours ago, when I was staggering along MLK, expecting to get shot by one of Stang's crew. Right now, I'll do anything to save my mom, and it's that sense of resolve that's giving me strength.

But it's also giving me a sense of urgency—I feel the clock ticking. I need to get moving, so I get down to practical matters. The only extra pants I have in here are those ridiculous black waiter pants that the Senate Dining Room staff wear. I decide to keep on my soggy cargos instead, ripped knees and all. But I do have some unused T-shirts lying around. I put on two dry Ts and feel like a new kid. I also put some fresh duct tape on the wires to keep them in place. It's a miracle they're still working.

Then I clean up my cuts with my old shirt, gritting my teeth as I use Listerine to clean out the wounds (it's the only antiseptic I have) and duct tape to cover the gash on my forearm (make that a million and two household uses for duct tape). At least it will keep it from opening up again. I'm sure if I went to a hospital they'd sew it up with a dozen stitches.

At first I shoulder my backpack, figuring I should keep it with me when I go to see Ms. Verita, but then I have second thoughts. I don't want anything to slow me down. The only reason to bring it is to be able to show Ms. Verita the original video files, but I have to assume she's already seen the copies I left in her office. Otherwise, she'd have no reason to want to see me again. I mean, she's the Legislative Director for the Majority Leader of the United States House of Representatives. She's too busy and important to care about me—especially now, with the big vote looming—unless she needs me. *I really have to get going.*

I stash my laptop under the cot mattress, grab my baseball cap and another empty pizza box (it's my last one), and head out the door, making sure I lock it tight. On a busy night like tonight, my pizza delivery boy outfit is the perfect disguise. Well, not perfect. I still look like I went a few rounds in the ring with Floyd Mayweather, Jr. But I wouldn't be the first beat-up-looking pizza guy. The only thing that would make me feel better is a sweatshirt since it's so cold outside—I really can't wear Dottie's. Not only is it soaked all the way through, but it's also shredded. She's going to kill me.

I cross the subbasement to the House side and climb one of the service stairwells that comes out just down the hall from H-107. I look like crap, but I feel good, all things considered, as I slip out of the stairwell door and into the hall.

"Gotcha, kid!"

The sound startles me. It must be that my bad eye is blinder than I thought, because the next thing I know, I feel two big hands grab me from that side.

It's Melon.

Before I can react, Melon yanks my arms behind my back, the pizza box hits the marble floor with a loud clap, and Chase straps a pair of plastic handcuffs on me. My heart's hammering—I've got to get to Ms. Verita. Getting bagged by the guards wasn't part of my plan.

"You're coming with me," Melon declares, gloating. He pulls me roughly down the hall toward the main entry of the building. I'm so surprised, angry, and scared that I don't have any of my usual sassy remarks ready for him.

I look up at Chase, who is trying to avoid eye contact.

"Happy birthday," I say, trying to sound feisty, but my delivery is flat.

Chase glares at me like I just called her a name, but she says nothing. Melon, however, smacks me in the back of the head and says, "Quiet, kid."

As we're passing over to the Senate side, he gets out his phone and speed-dials a number. He's keeping his voice low, so I can barely hear him. He utters a few "Yes, sirs," so I'm guessing he's talking to Rhino, especially since we're heading in the direction of the guard station.

While he's talking, my mind is racing. How did Melon and Chase catch me? It's like they were lying in wait. I mean, I just saw them on video surveillance in the guard station, eating cupcakes. Are they tracking me? Do they know where my suite is? I'm starting to feel paranoid, but I don't want to show it.

After he finishes the conversation and stashes his phone, Melon takes more of an interest in me. "Looks like someone else caught up with you before I did," Melon says, examining my face. "That's what happens to lying little thieves."

"Nah, it was a nasty cat," I say. "Pets are a hazard."

Chase chuckles, but Melon doesn't think it's funny. He smacks me in the head again. "Go on, kid, keep making fun. But this is the end of the line for you. You're done for. What you got there," he points to my swollen eye, "is going to seem like a cat *scratch* if you don't keep your mouth shut."

He doesn't know it, because I'd never let it show, but every time he smacks me in the head, he hits one of my bumps and I see stars.

Turns out we're not going to the guard station after all. Instead, we stop at the subway and wait with a few staffers for the next train. When we start getting some looks, Melon announces, "Routine security matter," and pulls me closer. Chase closes in to hide me from the staffers.

I always wanted to ride on the private subway. The cars are like glass-enclosed booths (I've heard the glass is bulletproof, but I hope not to test it—at least not tonight). The train moves faster than I thought it would as it whisks us over to the Senate administrative offices.

There are even more politicians and staffers waiting at the station there to take the train back to the Capitol. Melon and Chase do their best to hide me, but I can tell that we're causing heads to turn and maybe a few concerned remarks.

When Chase pushes *3* on the elevator control panel, I know exactly where I'm being taken.

Looks like Rhino and his brutes have been colluding with Julien. If I can record all of this and get out alive, I'll be able to nab two birds with one stone, as they say. A lot of ifs, I know. Despite my circumstances, I'm feeling good about my odds. After all, it's still my *lucky* day (I hope).

But as soon as we walk into Julien's office and the door closes, my heart sinks. Seeing Julien sitting behind his desk with that smug look on his face (he's not actually looking at me; he's doing the laptop thing) makes me feel like my luck's run out. With Stang, at least, you know what you're up against. He's a ruthless killer—a lion that attacks head-on. Julien is a snake, lying in the grass, coiled and waiting to strike. I have a feeling he could kill someone and they wouldn't even know it until after they were dead and haunting a place.

When I was crouched under the Senate subway just a little while ago, he was in Senator Charles's office. How did he get back here before us? I'm starting to think they set a trap for me. Someone must have seen me on video moving around in the tunnels. Guess I must have overlooked a few hidden cameras.

"Well, well," Julien says, clacking away on his keyboard and not looking up from his monitor, "look what the cat dragged in."

"Funny, we were just talking about cats," I say, and this time I pull off the playful tone I was striving for earlier.

Chase smirks, then quickly covers it up.

Julien looks up from his screen and glowers at Chase. (He's the only guy I know who has the glowering thing down.)

Melon tells Chase to wait outside and guard the door. Chase knows she's being dismissed, but she almost looks relieved. She hurries out the door.

"Tie him up," Julien commands with a flap of his hand, and then returns to his keyboard and laptop. While he's supposedly attending to his important Congressional business (which, I'm sure, is true because he's got to be certain his ducks are lined up for tomorrow's vote), Melon gets out the duct tape and proceeds to strap me back into the very same chair I had escaped from only the day before. In fact, there are still bits of tape stuck to the chair arms and legs. I would be laughing right now at the irony, if I didn't have such a powerful sense of déjà vu and alarming memories of being stuck in Julien's closet, waiting to die.

"There," Melon says. Then he punches me in the

head—right above my bad eye—for good measure. An evil grin creases his square face.

Both my eye and nose start bleeding. The blood dribbles down my chin onto my shirt.

Julien looks up. "Let's hope that won't be necessary again, Decker."

Melon nods, then steps behind me, but I can tell he's still in arm's reach and itching to unload again. Plus, I think that Julien was speaking to him in code. I'm pretty sure he meant: "I can't wait for you to clobber the little punk again."

Julien opens a drawer to his desk, pulls a couple of things out, and holds them up. It's my Passport hard drive and Black Beauty. I can feel my stomach doing flips. But I remind myself that I wanted to get to Julien tonight, so I should consider myself fortunate (see, it *is* my lucky day). Besides, I expected the Passport to end up in Julien's hands eventually (Black Beauty was a goner from the moment I left her behind), and I knew it wouldn't be easy to get a confession out of him.

I swallow hard and try to imagine LaQuota sitting in her kitchen, listening in on this exchange while it's being recorded. I want to make LaQuota proud.

"Where did you get this?" Julien says, holding up the Passport. His voice is thin and dangerous.

I shrug. "Can't remember exactly," I say, "but I used it to copy those boring documentaries from your servers."

Julien narrows his eyes at me then flicks his head at Melon.

Melon hauls off and socks me on the side of the head. I feel my neck crunch, but it sounds worse than it feels. I wag my head to clear it. "Why did you have Melon punch me?"

"Melon?" Julien says. He smirks. He likes my nickname for Decker.

"Because, little urchin, you're disrespecting me, which means you're disrespecting Senator Charles, and we can't have that."

He nods at Melon again. I try to brace myself, but it's hard when you can't see which side the blow is coming from. He catches me in my swollen eye again and it starts gushing. Blood streams down my face. That time I saw stars. I won't be able to take too many more of these, so I need to figure out how to get Julien to admit to owning those servers.

"Must have taken you a long time to gather all of those, uh, home movies," I say. "It's a pretty impressive library."

Julien nods again, but this time I'm ready. I plant my feet on the floor and push back with all my might, launching myself and my chair right into Melon's groin. He staggers back and slams into the door and I fall over flat on my back. Fortunately, the floor is carpeted, or I might have knocked myself out.

Chase pushes the door open and peeks in. "Everything OK in here?" She frowns at Melon kneeling to the side, holding his groin.

Julien is irate by now. He gets up, comes over, kicks me in the side of the head, and then stands my chair up again.

"You two, wait outside," he commands Melon and Chase.

I'm feeling a little woozy at this point, but I still have

enough of my senses to try one more time with Julien. When the door closes, I say, "If anything happens to me, all of the videos on that disk will be going live on YouTube tomorrow."

That stops Julien for a moment. He studies me for a moment, then says, "You're bluffing."

I guess by the look on my face that he can tell I meant what I said, because he adds, "And even if you're not, there's no way to link those videos to me. I'm too clever for that."

When he says those words, my heart starts hammering. Is that the evidence I'm looking for? It seems so subtle, and yet, in some sense, he just admitted that he knows about the videos.

"We'll see," I say.

Just then, there's a soft knock at the door. Julien seems to know who it is, because he immediately jumps to open it. My back is to the door, so I can't see who's coming in until he shuffles past my chair.

If my jaw didn't hurt so bad, it probably would have dropped. It's Senator Charles.

SENATOR CHARLES

All I can think when I see Senator Charles settle into the chair in front of Julien's desk is: *this really must be my lucky day!* I'm pretty confident that I just bagged Julien with my wire, and now I might even get the kingpin, too! But I feel like crap and don't know how long I can last. At least Melon is outside, so I won't be getting any more of those Godzilla-sized punches to the head.

As soon as Senator Charles clears his throat and starts to speak, I realize there's a reason he's a senator and Julien's just his Chief of Staff. His voice, while old and gravelly, also has a soft, silken tone and a mesmerizing lilt. It's decades of giving thunderous speeches, wooing big donors, conning voters, and sucking up to the media that make his Capitol Charm so impressive. Just by his captivating tone and cadence, I feel like there will be no implicating him in the illegal surveillance videos. He's much too shrewd.

"The boy from the dining room," Senator Charles says

in a voice that rings with grand oratory timbre, like he's the emcee at the Grammies. He has an amused look on his face, and a gleam in his old eyes, but I can tell that he's not really amused.

He's sitting hunched over, but since he was once such a tall man, he's still looking at me eye to eye. His thick shock of white hair is neatly groomed, as are his eyebrows, although a few strands poke out like little white inchworms.

By its sheen and perfect cut, I'm guessing his navy blue suit is expensive, although it's a bit crumpled on account of his bent posture. But I can see where Julien gets his taste for crimson ties, because that's what Senator Charles has on, only his seems to have some kind of paisley pattern lightly etched into it, whereas Julien goes for straight-up crimson. If Julien were a vampire, he'd drink his blood warm where Senator Charles might throw in an ice cube or two. Maybe those two like to cool their heels in The Crypt.

Senator Charles twirls his cane absently between his fingers.

He sees me looking at the cane now and begins to chuckle, low and deep. Quicker than he looks capable, he thrusts the cane in my direction—not to strike me, but to let me see it up close.

"It's pretty, isn't it, boy?" he says, twisting it so I can get a good look at the ornate gold handle. It's just a knob on the end, like the stick shift of Ant-Man's car (Ant-Man would kill to have a gold handle like that on his Mazda), and the shaft is thick, really thick. More like a weapon than a walking stick. And it's glossy and stained really dark. At first, I thought it was black. There's a gold tip (or maybe it's brass, but probably gold) fitted on the end to protect the wood from wear and tear.

I don't say anything. I don't even nod. I'm still trying to figure out this wily old coyote, and fast. He can clearly see I'm in bad shape, and that some unsavory things have been going down in Julien's office, but he's chosen not to acknowledge any of it, almost as if he's used to this kind of scene.

He pulls the cane back and examines the handle. "This cane has history," he says. "It's the very cane that Brooks used to beat the living daylights out of that traitor, Sumner." The light in Senator Charles's eyes flashes when he says this.

I frown. "I thought Brooks's cane was in a museum in Boston." I'm lisping because my lip is so swollen.

Senator Charles studies me. I can tell that I've surprised him. He looks mildly impressed. "That's the official story. But the one in Boston is a replica—just one of many. This is the original." He holds the cane out again for me to see.

"If it was me, I'd rather have an original Jackie Robinson bat," I say, grinning a little. It hurts to grin too much.

Senator Charles chuckles again, a sadistic sound that seems to draw its resonance from the earth, maybe even from hell. "You have pluck, boy, and that's admirable."

But that's it for compliments, because what he says next is meant to rattle me. "But once a criminal, always a criminal." He leans forward and stares at me with serpent eyes, daring me to respond. I know he's taunting me, and I should just let it go, but I can't help myself. First, I roll my eyes. Actually, I roll my *eye*; the other one's so swollen shut it doesn't count. Then I say, "Couldn't have said it better myself."

Those clear blue eyes see pretty well, because Senator Charles doesn't like my response. His mouth twitches. It's a grimace, a subtle one, but I catch it, and Julien does, too.

Julien responds on cue: he slaps me across the face. (Slaps!) "Show the senator respect," he seethes.

"That's enough," Senator Charles says, as if he's the beneficent god who has the power to punish or show mercy. He sits up as straight as his bent old body will allow. "What's your name, son?"

I look him square in the eyes and say, "Kid."

Senator Charles snorts. "Is that spelled with one *D* or two?" He chuckles at his own joke. I hadn't even thought of the pirate reference before—Captain Kidd—but it's a good one. I'll have to remember that. There's also Billy the Kid, famous outlaw. Maybe Senator Charles should have asked me if my first name was Billy.

But he continues before I can come up with a smart retort. "Well, *Kid*, I must say that I am impressed by your ability to elude full-grown men—the hapless Capitol Police who allegedly defend these grounds—with apparent ease. And, based on the reports I've heard," he looks from me to Julien and back again, "you have quite a unique skill set. What grade are you in?"

"I don't go to school. It's worthless."

"Precisely!" Senator Charles declares, as if I've just made a very important point for him. But I don't know what point I've made. He sees my confusion and chuckles.

"For children like you, school *is* worthless," he says, lifting his cane and rolling it between his fingers. "There's no point in wasting taxpayer dollars on a child who will never be more than a common criminal or drug addict."

Now I really can't hold back. I swear at the old buzzard, using choice curses. Who does he think he is calling me a criminal when he's the one committing the really big crimes? And his comment about drug addicts strikes too close to home. I know he meant to hurt me, to get me riled up, but I can't help myself. I strain against my duct tape bonds as if I would hit him.

Julien slaps me again. I turn and spit at him. He raises his hand to retaliate, but Senator Charles does the beneficent god thing with his cane.

"You realize, of course, that you are simply proving my point with every word you utter." He sits back and examines the gold handle of his cane again. "Let me ask you, *Kid*, do you have a job?"

At first I don't want to answer him, but then I decide I might as well. But I also know that I can't give him too many details. For all I know, LaQuota is listening to this exchange live, as it streams in to her shop. She would kill me if I mentioned Come Up. "Sometimes," I say.

"Running drugs?" Julien sneers.

Senator Charles raises a hand to Julien as if to say, *I'll do the questioning.*

"What would you say if I told you I could get you a real job with a reputable company?" he asks.

"Depends on the pay and the company." Because Ms. Verita explained The Dummies Act to me, I think I know where he's going with this.

Senator Charles chuckles. "What if I said that instead of learning *worthless* subjects in school, you could learn a trade *and* get paid?"

I smile. "Some trades are *worthless*, too. What trade?"

Senator Charles's eyes flash. He has only so much patience for my sass. "You like computers, don't you?"

I shrug.

"Instead of algebra, you could learn how to build computers."

"Build as in *design*? Or build as in snap the parts together on an assembly line?" I say, recalling Ms. Verita's explanation about cheap labor and mindless jobs.

"You may be smart, *Kid*, but you're not smart enough to design a computer." Senator Charles's eyes flash again. "To quote one of the masterminds of our age, Charlie Munger—do you know who he is?"

I shake my head.

"He's the former Vice Chairman of Berkshire Hathaway," Senator Charles says with great reverence. "A true financial genius. He once said that 'even an institution like McDonald's is one of the most successful educational institutions in the United States. They take people and give them a first job, which helps them get a second job. They do a very, very good job of taking troubled youth and making model citizens.'"

I laugh. It reminds me of my first conversation with Ms. Verita about Senator Charles. "You sound a lot like Ebenezer Scrooge to me." I lower my voice to try to make it sound like Scrooge's in that scene where the men come around to collect donations for the poor. "Are there no prisons, no work houses?" I wag my finger at the senator. He's not amused.

I can feel Julien's hand levitating behind me, but Senator Charles shakes him off. He studies me some more. I think he's trying to work out how much I know. Or maybe he's trying to figure out if I'm worthy of a response. After a few long moments, he takes the bait.

"It is not one such as you, *Kid*, who advances civilization, gives rise to high culture, or builds new industries. It is the aristocracy. Sadly, during my long tenure in the Senate, I have watched America surrender more and more of the rights of its aristocracy to prop up *worthless* citizens like you." Senator Charles pauses.

I'm starting to regret having brought up the word *worthless*.

"My colleagues on the other side of the aisle," the great senator continues as if he's addressing his fellow senators rather than a thirteen-year-old kid, "call the empowerment of the middle and lower classes *democracy* when it's really nothing more than *socialism*. And socialism will be the death of America's primacy in the world, as it was for the Soviet Union."

He pauses and leans forward again, shaking the handle of his cane at me. "The stakes, *Kid*, have never been greater. We are engaged in a battle for the future of our great country." Senator Charles turns his oratory prowess way up. His voice trills with conviction. "Even as foreign powers arise abroad to threaten us economically and politically—such as the Asian nations, and someday Latin American—we fall further behind. As my final act, I have a plan to transform our great land so that even little crooks like you can be productive and contribute to our future, rather than being the drag on American society that you are." He pauses. Clearly, he's practicing some kind of speech, although I'm sure this is not the official version. Quietly, he adds, "The time has come for Real Reform."

I know he's referring to his legislation. I glance at Julien, who has this moist, fawning look in his eyes, like he's just heard the voice of God.

"Oh, you mean The Dummies Act," I say, doing my best to smirk at the great senator. He's so smug, talking down to me, it ticks me off; but I don't want him to see that he's getting under my skin. "Maybe you can clear something up for me about that." It's hard to speak clearly since my lip's so swollen and I have to keep sucking in my saliva. "Is it called The Dummies Act because it was written by a bunch of dummies, or is it that the American people are dummies, or that they should be turned into dummies? Or maybe it's all of those?" I try to sustain my grin while I stare at Senator Charles.

My jab doesn't penetrate the old senator's crusty shell. He knows he's the man in control and there's no way he lets a punk like me rattle him.

He studies me with those cold blue eyes, and then turns to Julien. "Clearly, you've underestimated him."

I realize that it's now or never if I'm going to try to implicate Senator Charles in Julien's illegal video surveillance scheme. "Has Julien told you about the home movies he's been making?" I say. "Maybe you guys plan to take your act to Hollywood when you're done here on Capitol Hill."

Without looking at me, which tells me I struck a nerve, he rises slowly from his chair, using his cane for support. I guess the silent treatment is the noble's way of brushing off *worthless* criminals like me.

Julien makes a move to assist him, but Senator Charles

waves him off.

As the old senator shuffles past me, he says to Julien, "Keep him safe until after the vote tomorrow. Then dispose of him." And with that, he disappears through the door.

GET OUT OF JAIL FREE, AGAIN

After Senator Charles is gone, Julien instructs Melon to gag me and stick me in the closet. My heart starts hammering when I hear Julien's instructions. For some reason, that dark closet scares the bejesus out of me. I guess it feels like a prelude to death. I escaped it once, but what are the odds I'll draw a Get Out of Jail Free card again? Truth is, I'm surprised Julien hasn't asked me how I escaped the first time. My guess is he probably knows, which makes me worry about Lana.

After giving his instructions, Julien leaves. It's down to me and Melon in the office. Chase, I think, is still standing guard outside. Melon knocks me around a bit, but not as bad as I expected, before stuffing a wad of paper in my mouth and slapping duct tape over it. The whole time he doesn't say anything to me, even when I make fun of him and tell him he made a mistake getting in bed with these jerks. It's as if Senator Charles gave the silent treatment order to everyone. When he's done taping me up, Melon drags me into the closet and shuts the door.

Because my nose is clotted with blood and maybe even broken, I'm having more trouble breathing than last time. I start to feel light-headed and I'm really panicking, but then a sense of calm comes over me unexpectedly. Well, not entirely unexpectedly, because I'm replaying in my head my conversation with Senator Charles, and I'm comparing it to what Ms. Verita had to say to me.

All I know is Ms. Verita was right when she talked about Rich Supremacists. Senator Charles made her point for her: if he has his way, he'll change the laws of the land to permanently strip the average kid of education, rights, and opportunity.

The way he looked at me, there was no doubt in his mind that I don't stand a chance of becoming anything more than a Have Not. He believes—I could see it in those stony blue eyes—he really believes that all men are not created equal. So why waste any time or money on a kid like me? Maybe I'm feeling calm because I know (hope) that my wire picked up Senator Charles's impromptu speech and transmitted it to LaQuota's server. It has to be good for something.

But sitting here all alone in the dark, my thoughts gravitate to my mom. Whether he was being shrewd or just lucky, Senator Charles hit a nerve. My mom's a drug addict—as bad as they come—but she wasn't always that way. I have a few good childhood memories that I cling to because they're all I have. When I was five and six years old, just after my dad was locked up the first time (his life sentence came a year or two later) and before the drugs got really bad, it was just me and my mom. She used to take me to the museums, and we'd walk down the Mall while she pointed out all the famous buildings and monuments. On our walks, she would build me up and tell me that I was smart as a whip, that she could see me working here one day, on the other side of the river. Maybe it's on account of those memories that I fled here when I knew I had to escape Stang. It wasn't a conscious decision to come to the Capitol, but maybe it was subconscious. I'd kind of forgotten some of those memories until now, sitting here all alone with a death sentence hanging over my head.

I love my mom, and she loves me. A tear runs down my cheek, and then another, and pretty soon I'm a waterworks. It's like my mom's already died and I'm mourning her. Or maybe it's that I know I'm going to die, and I'm mourning my pathetic life. Either way, I'm surprised as heck when the closet door suddenly opens and the office light blinds me.

It takes my one good eye a moment to focus through the tears and bright light, but I figure out pretty quick that it's Chase. I cringe, expecting that maybe she heard me carrying on and came in from the hall to shut me up. Instead, she drags my chair out of the closet and grabs a box of tissues off Julien's desk. She dabs my face lightly, wiping away tears and blood.

"I don't know what you did, kid, but these guys intend to kill you. I didn't sign up for that." She starts to remove the duct tape while she's talking, saving the mouth gag for last. Maybe she's afraid I'll shout out or something. Or maybe she just wants to say her piece without me interrupting, because she keeps talking in a nervous stream.

"Decker just asked me if I wanted to have some fun, it being my birthday and all. He said he had figured out how to catch the Capitol Kid—that's what we call you around here." She smiles at me, but then continues with a serious look. "But Decker's caught up in something bigger and I don't want to get involved. I can't afford to lose this job, you know what I mean?" With that, she rips the duct tape off my mouth and I spit out the wad of paper.

I take a deep breath—it feels good to fill my lungs—then I say, "I know exactly what you mean."

"Well," Chase says, standing back as if to give me room to get up and go, "you seem like a smart kid, and, frankly speaking, we all appreciate your little pranks on the senators and congressmen. These people are so full of themselves they could use a little cutting down to size now and then. That's why Lonnigan never really called in the FBI or tried too hard to catch you." She pauses and smiles again. I've never seen this side of Chase before. She seems nice. "But this is serious, kid, and if I were you, I'd be taking the express train out of here. And I don't just mean this Capitol Building; I mean DC. Somehow you got mixed up with a senator, and that can't be good."

I reach out and take Chase's hand. At first she flinches, a natural security guard response, but then she lets me take it. "Thanks," I say. "And I'm going to take your advice, but I got one more prank to pull before I go."

"Are you crazy? Didn't you hear me? They mean to kill you!"

When she sees I'm not going to change my mind, Chase shakes her head, but then she grins. "Wish I could see it, but I'm getting out of here. My shift ended an hour ago and I don't see the point of sticking around even though Decker asked me to. You're on your own, kid."

I wink at Chase, squeeze her hand, then crack open the door. The coast is clear—kind of. There are a few staffers at the other end of the hall, but I'm not going that way. I turn back to Chase and say, "I owe you one," and then I dart out the door and into the stairwell.

RAPPELLING

Ms. Verita must be wondering what happened to me. While I'm bounding down the stairs three at a time, I pull my smartphone from my cargo pocket. Melon was gloating too much when he caught me to think of searching me, or he would have taken my phone and maybe found the wire, too. I'm surprised when I don't see any texts from Ms. Verita, but I'm sure she's preoccupied with preparations for tomorrow. I've learned a lot about how Congress works (and doesn't) while I've been here. Since Ms. Verita's the Legislative Director and Representative Bridges is Democracy First's sponsor, it's up to Ms. Verita and her staff to write the bill. I'm sure they're working like crazy with changes from last-minute negotiations.

I decide not to text her. It's probably better if I just get over there and tell her everything that's happened. Senator Charles looked pretty confident that his Real Reform—The Dummies Act—was going to pass. And that worries me. If Julien's a snake, Senator Charles is the Devil (I think my Garden of Eden analogy ends there, because the Capitol is no Eden—or is it?).

When I told Chase I had one last prank up my sleeve, I meant my hidden wire. I need to see if those recordings I got are any good and share them with Ms. Verita. If it worked, there has to be a way to take down Julien and maybe even Senator Charles.

When I get to the basement level where the subway runs to the Senate side, I make for the service door that leads beneath the subway. As I'm sprinting down the tunnel, I hear the subway rumble overhead. Too bad my one and only trip on the subway was with Melon and Chase.

By the time I get to the Capitol Building, I have a plan. It's not a very good one, I know, but it will have to do. It's obvious to me that security is going to be crawling all over the place. Not only is Congress working overtime tonight, but I suspect that Rhino and his guards are on edge. Fortunately, they think I'm locked up. But I'm pretty sure Melon will be back to check on me, and when he finds Chase gone and me missing, all hell will break loose.

Unfortunately, I'm guessing that they've been looking through old video surveillance to track my movements. It won't be hard to connect me with Ms. Verita, and that means Representative Bridges. I might be overthinking this—and I hope I am—but it pays to be paranoid around here.

There's only one way I can come up with to get to Representative Bridges's office without getting stopped and ending up in handcuffs again, and that means taking the roof. The trouble is getting down from the roof, but I have a crazy thought for that, too. I make a pit stop in one of the janitor closets and grab two large extension cords that I drape over each shoulder to balance myself.

The cords are heavy, and I'm pretty much shot at this point, with all my narrow escapes and near-death experiences on this, my *lucky* day, but my adrenaline's working overtime—it's the cornered prey syndrome. I've been in a corner so long today, that pure adrenaline is flowing through my veins. I'm no longer the prey; I'm the predator.

I get to the top of the stairs and ease open the door to the roof. When Congress is busy like it is tonight, they usually put Capitol Police up here. But it's cold out tonight and there's a mixture of drizzle, sleet, and snow in the air, which means that if there are security guards, they're not walking the roof; they're keeping to their posts.

The coast looks clear. I take my path along the roof that keeps me out of sight of the surveillance cameras. I don't know exactly where H-107 is, but the balconies that run along the complex of offices are so long, I have a big margin of error. I just need to land on Representative Bridges's.

I drop the extension cords at the edge of the roof and rub my shoulders to get the blood flowing again. While I'm squatting there, trying to figure out my next move, I find it hard to believe that just beneath my feet an epic battle is under way: Real Reform versus Democracy First.

But my gaze is drawn to the city lights. To the Smithsonian, the Washington Monument, Lincoln Memorial, the White House—I can even catch a glimpse of the National Cathedral from here in between fast-moving, low-slung clouds that are still spitting out a frozen mist. It all looks so serene and surreal, like a life-sized snow globe.

It occurs to me that it's the blood, sweat, and tears of the ordinary people that made all this possible. And it's the belief in ordinary people that gives these grand structures their majesty. If that's not noble, I don't know what is. I figure that Senator Charles's vision of nobility is really just a lame excuse to defend money and power. If you're at the top of the pecking order, you'll do anything to stay there.

It can't be that the circumstances of your birth determine your rights. That's just too cruel for anyone with half a brain to believe, and that's the flaw the founding fathers of America were trying to fix. Their vision was a level playing field. That makes sense to me. And that's worth fighting for.

But I don't have time now to contemplate founding philosophies. Besides, I don't know enough to know if I'm right or wrong or if history's on my side. But I do know that if I get out of this jam, I might pick up a book or two and try to figure it out.

Right now, though, I wish I had a book on rappelling. It looks like a long way down when I lie flat on my stomach and peek over the edge of this roof.

I grit my teeth (which hurts—I think one of my molars is loose) and look around for a way to secure the extension cords. There's a two-way brass fire hydrant nearby that looks to me like it's anchored well enough to hold my weight. I wrap the end of one of the cords around it and tie it as tight as I can. Then I connect the extension cords using a knot to prevent them from unplugging on me in mid-air.

I toss the free end of the second cord over the edge of the roof. I expect to hear it hit something, which would tell me it's long enough, but I don't hear anything. Not good. But I have to believe it will get me close enough to my destination that I can drop the rest of the way without killing myself.

After testing the cord a couple of times, I try to pump myself up to go over the roof, but my knees start to go soft every time I get close to the edge. I know I jumped out a third-story window a few hours ago, but I didn't have time to think about it.

Before now, I've had thoughts of skydiving because to me, skydiving seems like flying. I'd love to fly. That's what I love about birds. They're so free. They come and go as they please: borders and boundaries, fences and gates, roads and sidewalks don't mean anything to them.

But now I know I'll never go skydiving. The bird thing will have to wait until I'm reincarnated or something. I mean, if I can't even rappel off this roof using a rope (OK, extension cord), there's no way I would jump out of a perfectly good plane!

"You can do this, Boot," I say, trying to psyche myself up. "For Ms. Verita." It's that last part that gives me the courage to let my feet drop over the edge. But I know right away I've made a mistake. I underestimated just how slick the cord would be with all this precipitation. I begin sliding down really fast, almost like I'm free-falling. No matter how hard I grip or squeeze my sneakers on the cord, I hardly slow down. So I just close my eyes and expect to break every bone in my body.

To my surprise, I hit something soft. It's not like the trash bags, which were piled high enough to cushion my fall and save me. Instead, it's a hard landing on a soft surface. Fortunately, by the time I hit, my efforts to slow myself down were starting to work.

But now I know why I didn't hear the cord hit something when I tossed it over the edge of the roof. It landed on one of the soft lounge chairs on the Speaker of the House's balcony. And it's that lounge chair that breaks my fall now.

Even though I was slowing down, I still hit the chair pretty hard, knocking it one way and me the other. I crash into a coffee table. Besides a really loud ruckus, I don't think I did anything worse to myself than dent another fender or two. And the furniture is sturdy cast-aluminum stuff, so all it does is scatter out of the way without breaking.

But I'm on the wrong balcony, and I made as much noise as a marching band. I can't afford to get caught again. So I grab the extension cord and pull it around to one of the giant columns and wrap it around the base. It's not the best hiding place, but since it's dark and wet out, you'd have to really be looking to see it. Someone will find it in the morning, but by then I'll be out of here…one way or another.

Just then, the balcony door opens and someone walks out to have a look around. I duck behind the column and hold my breath. As I expected, they don't see the extension cord, and don't seem to notice the disrupted furniture. There's a lot of furniture on this balcony, so it might just look like someone pulled some chairs around for a meeting or to catch an afternoon ray while taking a catnap. Speaker Landon is famous for taking catnaps, even when he's up on the podium in the House Chamber for all to see. The media likes to make fun of him.

After a few minutes, whoever it was returns inside and latches the door.

When I'm alone again, I try to figure out my options. There's really only one, and it's not good. I have to crawl along the wet and slippery ledge to Representative Bridges's offices and balcony.

Now I really do need to be a predator. I need to be a cat.

THE ART OF WAR

*T*he only good news about this ledge is that it's only a couple of stories up and I see grass down there, which means that as long as I don't break my neck, I'll probably survive a fall. Other than that, it's too narrow for my feet and it's slick as ice. But somehow, I'm holding on.

Senator Scrooge might see me as a lowly, good-for-nothing criminal, but what he doesn't know is that I might be an expert rock climber someday—especially if I make it across this ledge!

I can't let myself get distracted making fun of Senator Charles or I'll be sure to slip, and that would really be ironic. There's no way I'm letting him have the last laugh.

I shuffle along an expanse of windowless wall between the Speaker's suite and the Majority Leader's. Fortunately, there's a narrow cut in the facade that I can dig my fingers into, and that saves me every time my feet slip. But now that I'm approaching the first window, my convenient fingerhold stops at an ornate stone frame that juts out and that I have to figure out how to get around.

It isn't pretty. I'm doing everything to reach my arm around the frame so I can grab on to something. My fingers find a protruding stone feature that feels secure, so I grab on and lunge around the frame. The problem is, my fingers are so tired, cold, and stiff they don't cooperate, and my lunge is a little too vigorous.

I lose my grip.

If I thought I had adrenaline pumping before, now it floods my system. I start flailing my arms and somehow catch hold of the lower latch on the window.

These windows are enormous—fifteen feet or more— so they have more than one latch, and I was lucky enough to grab the very last one. I'm holding on, but I can also feel my grip slipping.

Someone inside must have heard me, because I can feel them trying to open the window. They're jiggling my latch, which is making my grip slip faster. The only thing I have going for me is that my feet seem to have found a nook, so I'm able to relieve the pressure on my hand and get a better hold. Fortunately, the jiggling stops, but I'm still on the verge of falling and there's no way I'm strong enough to pull myself up.

Just then, the window next to me, which is about five feet away, opens and someone pokes their head out.

I know I've said it's my lucky day, but I've had my doubts until right now—of all people to look out the window, it's Ms. Verita! When she sees me, she screams. It's not the kind of scream like, "Burglar! Burglar!" It's more like fear for a friend's life.

"Boot! ¿Eres tu?" she cries. She knows it's me, but what else are you going to say when someone you know is about to plunge two stories to their death and you just see them for the first time.

Another head pokes out of the window behind Ms. Verita. I don't have time to respond before Ms. Verita springs to action.

"Hold on, Boot!" she cries. "We'll get you."

I don't know how Ms. Verita plans to get me. They can't open the window I'm holding on to without knocking me off, and I'm too far from Representative Bridges's balcony to stage a rescue. I start to look down to see if I can calculate the best way to land without breaking every bone in my body.

It seems like it takes Ms. Verita forever, and I don't know how much longer I can hold on. Finally, she returns with two big guys and a curtain that she must have torn down from a window.

"Boot, óyeme," Ms. Verita says, using her calm, convincing voice. "Listen closely. John is going to toss one end of this curtain to you. You're going to grab it and hold on for your life. Mack's holding the other end. John and Mack will pull you up. Do you understand?"

I nod. I'm afraid that if I speak, I might lose my grip. I'm that close to falling.

John must have some experience with curtain tossing because on his first try, he lands one end of it on my head. All I have to do is let go of the window latch, grab it, and hold on. It sounds easy to trust that John and Mack won't drop me—but it's not easy. Not at all. Lucky day or not.

Ms. Verita's standing in front of my window. She taps

it with her fingers. "Grab it, Boot." Her voice is muffled by the glass.

"For you, Ms. Verita," I whisper. Then I close my eyes, grab the curtain, and let go.

I don't think either John or Mack expected me to swing so far the other way because I feel myself slip and I hear a loud grunt. But I have to give them credit—they hold on and pull me up just as Ms. Verita promised. John (or maybe it's Mack) grabs me by the collar of my shirt and pulls me in headfirst through the window.

When I land on the floor and roll over onto my back, there are at least a dozen people gathered around. Some of them start clapping. John and Mack take a bow.

But Ms. Verita is not paying attention to any of them. Her focus is on me. She drops to my side and I can see her concern.

"¡Dios mío! Boot, what happened to you?" she gasps.

Before I can answer, she stands up and takes charge.

"OK, show's over, everyone. Clear out of this conference room. Now!" Her final command sends them scurrying.

"Emily," she says to a young looking girl, "bring me a first-aid kit. You'll find one in the bathroom. Hurry!"

When it's down to me and Ms. Verita, she inexplicably starts crying. I mean sobbing. "Boot," she says, stroking my face. "Ay, Boot, lo siento mucho. How did this happen? What did they do to you?" She keeps stroking my face.

I know I look like crap, but her reaction seems a little over the top to me. Just then, Emily returns with the first-aid kit. Ms. Verita thanks her and dismisses her.

"I want to know what happened," she says, regaining

her composure. "Everything. I want to know everything. They're not going to get away with this!" She's gone from blubbering to angry in the span of a minute. "This is Congress! This is not a ghetto where things get settled with knives and guns!" She's been fiddling with the zipper on the first-aid kit, but when she makes this last statement, she throws the kit down and hides her face in her hands. She's trying not to cry, but she can't help it.

"I'll be OK, Ms. Verita," I say, sitting up and reaching out to her. Suddenly, she wraps her arms around me and hugs me, hard, like if she let go, something bad would happen.

"Está bien, Ms. Verita," I say again, speaking more softly. Something else is going on here that I can't figure out.

Ms. Verita nods her head and wipes tears from her face.

"You know," she says, "that was very clever of you to figure out my codes. I knew you would. I just knew it."

I grin. That's more like the Ms. Verita I know. "Yeah, but you had me stumped for a while. At first I thought maybe Julien had one of his trojans on your phone, and that's why I was getting those codes."

"I think he does have some kind of tracker on my phone," Ms. Verita says. "It's been acting funny, kind of like my laptop. So I've been really cautious with my texts. I didn't want to put you in any danger." Her gaze drops to the floor. "A lot of good that did."

"Look, Ms. Verita," I say, taking her hand. "I feel like I was dragged across the potholes on MLK, and everything hurts, but not as bad as my conscience. I didn't..." I hesitate. "I mean, I haven't been straight with you. You need to know what's going on. I mean—"

Ms. Verita straightens up immediately. She's on full alert. "What *do you mean*, Boot?"

"I mean that I snuck into Julien's office a few days ago to get those videos I told you about."

Ms. Verita glares at me. She's hurt, I can tell, but not that hurt, which gives me the courage to go on.

"And while I was there, I kind of got stuck in the closet and overheard some things. I should have told you, but I was afraid you'd be mad at me. And then…well, even though you told me not to, I had to go back again. You see, I accidentally left…" My voice trails off.

Now Ms. Verita does look mad. "What are you saying?"

Just then, there's a knock on the door and Representative Bridges pokes her head in. She sees me and Ms. Verita sitting and kneeling on the floor.

"Is everything OK in here, Lucy?"

Ms. Verita nods. "Come in, Terry. I want you to meet someone."

Ms. Verita scrambles to her feet and pulls me to mine. "This is Boot, the boy I've been telling you about."

Representative Bridges walks over to shake my hand. She has a firm grip that seems to be measuring mine. My fingers are too stiff to return the favor. She eyes me in a suspicious, but not unfriendly, way—more like she's concerned for Ms. Verita.

"Nice to meet you, ma'am," I say, nodding my head.

"Nice to meet you, too, Boot. That's an interesting name. I'd like to hear all about it, but we have a busy night ahead of us." She pauses and takes a closer look at me. "You look like you need some medical attention. What happened here, Lucy?"

But I cut off Ms. Verita's response and address Representative Bridges directly. "I'll be OK, ma'am. But it's on account of your busy night that I came to pay Ms. Verita a visit. You see, I was just talking to Senator Scrooge—I mean, Charles."

The look I get from Representative Bridges and Ms. Verita is so comical, it makes me laugh. It's a combination of disbelief and belief that suspends their faces in some kind of mime state.

"This is no laughing matter, son," Representative Bridges says.

"I know. Believe me, I know." Then I point to my face and my soaked clothes as evidence of how much I get her point.

The three of us take a seat at the small conference table, and I tell them everything. I don't hold back. I mean, I'm only a thirteen-year-old kid (who might not make it to fourteen), and I don't have any agenda other than to stay out of juvie and get some help for my mom. The whole time I'm talking they don't interrupt. Not once. When I'm done, Representative Bridges says softly, "Do you still have the videos?"

I nod. "Yeah. I don't have all of them, because Julien's got the hard drive, but I have some on my laptop, which is back in my suite—I mean my room in the subbasement."

Representative Bridges can't suppress a grin when I accidentally say the word *suite*.

"But I gave copies to Ms. Verita." We both turn to her. She blushes, then reaches into her bra and pulls out the SD cards I had slipped in the envelope.

"I found them just before coming over here this afternoon," she says, trying to hide her embarrassment. "I haven't had a chance to look at them."

Although I don't show it, I'm surprised by Ms. Verita's comment. If she hasn't seen the videos yet, then why all the concern for me? It doesn't make sense, unless she really does believe me (maybe she really does like me, too?). Rather than make me feel good, that last thought worries me. It's like I don't want to disappoint her. More than ever. It's like I'm afraid to fail. It's like I *do* have something to lose: a true friend. But, like I said, I try not to show any of these feelings.

Without saying anything, I pop one of the cards into my smartphone and let Representative Bridges and Ms. Verita watch. They can't seem to get enough—they watch all of the videos on one card and then some from the second card, fast-forwarding through scenes they know. They watch video after video, including the one I saw with their negotiation strategy for Democracy First.

Finally, Representative Bridges says, "I've seen enough." Then she drums her fingers on the table and asks, "But how do we connect Senator Charles with all this?"

"Well, there's the wire I told you about." I grin and pull up my shirt to show them the duct tape and wire. "We can make a call to see if this," I point to my face as evidence, "was worth it. I mean, some of it came from the street—"

"I still can't believe you went back in there, Boot, to get a confession." Ms. Verita's eyebrows shoot up like they want to leave her face. "For an intelligent boy, that wasn't very smart!"

"Well, I was kind of *escorted* there, but that was lucky for us. And anyway, el loro viejo no aprende a hablar," I say, smiling. It was one of my mom's favorite sayings: you can't teach an old parrot how to talk. It's like the English version: you can't teach an old dog new tricks.

Ms. Verita doesn't think it's so funny. She shakes her head. "You're more like a mule than an old parrot. You risked too much."

Representative Bridges narrows her eyes at me, as if reconsidering her first impression. Then she starts to nod slowly, addressing Ms. Verita while watching me. "But it was clever, Lucy. And courageous."

"And stubborn!" Ms. Verita adds. "And thick-headed, and—"

Representative Bridges cuts Ms. Verita off. She wants to develop a battle plan. "What was the name of your friend who has the audio from that wire?" she asks.

When I told them my story, I mentioned LaQuota and her shop, but I tried to downplay that part. In her line of work, LaQuota doesn't like to attract attention. But Representative Bridges doesn't miss a trick.

"La-Quot-a," I say, making the shape of a capital *L* and quotes with my fingers.

Representative Bridges arches her eyebrows and shakes her head. I can tell she hasn't heard a name like that before. But she keeps on asking questions like she's feeling really pressed for time. "And you said La-Quot-a," she enunciates each syllable as if she's committing them to memory, "has a shop in Southeast. What was the name of her shop?"

I hadn't told her the name. That would have been too much detail. But there's no point trying to protect

LaQuota now. Besides, LaQuota told me that she always wanted to mess with a senator. Well, now's her chance.

"Come Up," I say.

Representative Bridges nods. "I want someone to go to Come Up and check out what's on those recordings. But," she adds, "I can tell you it won't be enough. Charles will hire high-priced attorneys who will claim fraud or entrapment or some similar defense. They'll try to sue us for libel. We'll need something more."

"Lana," I say. "And Chase."

"Who's Chase?"

I forgot they don't know my names for the guards.

"She works for Lonnigan, right, Boot?" Ms. Verita says, helping me out.

I nod.

"We're never going to get all of this evidence together by tomorrow morning," Representative Bridges says. She drums her fingers on the table again. I notice then that her fingers don't clack. I get a good look at her hands. Short fingernails and her hands look like working hands. I'm impressed.

"What are you thinking, Terry?" Ms. Verita asks after a short lull.

"I'm thinking that it will be better if Charles believes things are going his way tomorrow. 'The art of war is deception.'" Now she's drumming her fingers faster. Then she stops, as if she's made up her mind about something.

She turns to Ms. Verita. "Lucy, I have to go see Landon. Why don't you send Mack with Boot over to the pawnshop. Tell Mack to stop in an emergency room on the way back to get Boot cleaned up. But make sure he gets us that audio first!"

I raise my hands and start shaking my head. "No way! There's no way I can go back to Come Up. Stang's looking for me. He'll be sure to have his crew out there. We need to call LaQuota or text her or something and ask her to meet us."

"Fine," Representative Bridges agrees. "Get it done." Just like that, she stands and leaves the room. But before closing the door, she leans back in, looks me square in the eyes (well, eye), and says in a soft, sincere voice, "Thank you, Boot. Do you have a real name?"

I hesitate. "It's Henry."

"Thank you, Henry."

As the door closes, I hear her chuckle and mutter to herself, "Senator Scrooge."

LIGHTNING STRIKES

I try calling and texting LaQuota, but she isn't responding, which, I tell Ms. Verita, is no surprise. LaQuota does things in her own good time. What I don't tell Ms. Verita is that Stang's probably already paid LaQuota a visit tonight, looking for me, which means LaQuota won't want to have anything to do with me until things cool off again. I just hope he hasn't burned her place down.

I tell Ms. Verita we might have to send someone over to Come Up without me, but it should wait until morning for LaQuota's sake (and mine).

Ms. Verita sees the sense in my reasoning, but since it means I won't be going anywhere with Mack, she insists on examining my cuts and bruises while we're waiting to hear back from LaQuota.

"'The art of war is deception,'" Ms. Verita tells me while she's cleaning me up with the first-aid kit, "is a famous quote from Sun Tzu. Have you heard of Sun Tzu,

Boot?" she asks.

I shake my head.

Ms. Verita stops dabbing my eye with a cotton ball and looks at me very seriously. It makes me squirm.

"You're going to need stitches here and—"

She hesitates, then surprises me by switching conversations midsentence.

"I'm sorry about before, Boot—about losing it on you when you came through that window. You see…" She hesitates and her voice gets real soft. "You remind me of my brother. He joined the Crips when he was about your age. Not long after, he staggered into our house late one night, bloody and beat up, looking just like you. Only…" Her voice falters, but she continues. "Only his injuries were graver. He didn't survive the ride to the ER. He was fifteen. Seeing you like that…it was too much for me."

"Thank you, Ms. Verita," I say, squeezing her hand to steady it. She's shaking. "But can I ask you something?"

"Of course, Boot." She smiles gently. It makes my heart melt into my shoes.

"Why did you come here? I mean, to see all these senators and congressman in action, they're just as bad as Crips and Bloods. Worse, if you ask me, because they get away with it in broad daylight."

Ms. Verita laughs. "I hadn't thought of Democrats and Republicans that way before, but I suppose on some level you're exactly right." She pauses for a minute while she thinks about her answer.

"Greed and corruption can't last forever, Boot. By their very nature, they are doomed to implode. While we may not be able to match the power that billions of dollars can

Capitol Kid

buy, we can be ready to seize our opportunity when the cracks appear in the Rich Supremacists' control. It's what happened with white supremacy in this country, and it will happen again. That's when the voice of the people will be heard." The way she looks at me makes my heart skip a beat. She's so genuine. The real deal. I would do anything for Ms. Verita.

"I believe, Boot, that if you can make a little difference here, you can make a big difference out there." She points out the window to the wide world beyond. "After my brother died, I came here to make a difference."

Just then, we hear a commotion out in the hall. There's a loud knock on the door, and then it flies open. Mack, John, and little Emily are trying to block the door, but they're shoved out of the way by Rhino, Melon, and a whole bunch of Capitol Police.

"There he is!" Melon shouts, pointing at me.

I leap to my feet and make a run for the window. It's a natural reaction to flee in the face of approaching predators.

Ms. Verita shouts, "No, Boot, you don't have to run."

But Melon pushes past her and pulls out his gun.

By now, I've backed up all the way to the window and shoved it open. I know Melon is going to kill me. He has to—I've got too much on him. I think Ms. Verita knows it, too, because she scrambles over the conference table and runs in my direction.

Melon flicks the safety on his gun and without hesitating fires just as I slide halfway out the window. Miraculously, his first shot misses, but that's when my luck runs out and lightning strikes (the bad kind), because Melon takes aim again and fires, only this time, Ms. Verita throws herself in front of me. I think I hear the bullet hit her. The impact spins her body in the air; she bangs her head on the edge of the windowsill and falls to the floor unconscious.

"No!" I shout in horror and anger. I jump back in the window and hurl myself at Melon. By now, Rhino has intervened. He steps between me and Melon and intercepts me. I think I hear my bones crunch as he wraps his thick arms around me in a stranglehold.

I can't tell what happens next because Rhino's blocking my view and dragging me across the room, but it seems to me like the Capitol Police guys are fighting each other. Either that or Representative Bridges's staff took up arms against them.

I don't know where this last surge of adrenaline comes from because I feel like I used up my daily allotment a long time ago, but I start writhing and squirming in Rhino's grasp like my life was on the line. "Get off me!" I shout, planting my feet and launching my head into Rhino's chest.

My simple move catches him by surprise. The big guard grunts and lets his grip slip. I lunge away from him. "Ms. Verita!" I cry. "Ms. Verita!"

But before I make it three steps, several Capitol policemen gang-tackle and smother me like I was a loose football on the field.

I can hardly breathe, but I hear Rhino bellowing at the guards to get off me. And he's barking orders to get medical help for Ms. Verita. A few minutes later, he's got me in handcuffs and, with the help of his police, escorts me out of the Majority Leader's suite.

"You're in trouble, kid," Rhino says to me when we're out in the hall. "I don't know what you got yourself into, but I intend to find out."

"It's not me," I say defiantly. "It's Melon! He's the—"

"Who's Melon?"

"I mean Decker," I say. "He's the crook. He's in on it."

"We'll see," Rhino says.

Rhino's response surprises me. I'd assumed he was in on it, too, colluding with Julien, but maybe it was just Melon. At the moment, none of it matters. All concern for myself and the stupid Dummies Act is suddenly and forcefully eclipsed by that image of Ms. Verita flying through the air to save me.

I start to cry. No, not cry, blubber. I have to give Rhino credit. He lets me carry on without saying a word. After a few turns in the halls, I know where he's taking me: the guards' station.

By the time we get there, I'm not crying anymore, but I'm a mess. Rhino leads me to a little white holding cell with a chair, a table, and a ring mounted on the wall just above the table. Without saying anything, he temporarily undoes my cuffs and then reattaches them and both my hands to the ring on the wall.

"That ought to hold even the Capitol Kid," he says. His voice is not gruff. We've got some kind of understanding going on that I don't understand. Maybe I misjudged him.

He steps out and closes the door, leaving me alone, which is just about the worst thing he could do. I'd rather be duking it out with the captain of the guards than with my own conscience. I just hope Ms. Verita's OK. I'll never forgive myself if—

Just then, I feel my phone vibrate in my cargo pocket. It makes me jump. Since I popped in a new SIM card at Come Up, there are only two people who know this number: Ms. Verita and LaQuota. I'd be glad to hear from either one of them right now. My guess is that it's not Ms. Verita.

Have you ever tried to get something out of a cargo pocket while your hands are cuffed to the wall? It's not easy. I climb up on the table and kneel down, hoping that I can jiggle the phone out. But I can't get enough of a bend in my knee to let gravity do the work. By now, the phone has stopped vibrating, but I still want to get it out. Maybe I can figure out how to call LaQuota back.

I test the strength of the ring on the wall. It seems like if I can shimmy up the wall with my hands between my legs, I can get myself upside down, which ought to be enough to get the phone to drop out onto the table. I'm halfway up the wall when the door opens.

"What do you think you're doing, kid?" It's Rhino. He's angry. "Get down from there!" He starts pulling me down, when Representative Bridges walks in.

"I'll take it from here, Captain Lonnigan," she tells Rhino.

Rhino makes sure I'm back in my seat before leaving us alone.

"Are you OK, Boot?" Representative Bridges asks. She places her hand on the side of my face and looks me over.

I nod. "Ms. Verita—"

"An ambulance came for Lucy, Boot. She was unconscious when they took her away, but her vitals seemed good. She's in very capable hands."

I nod gratefully. "I'm sorry, ma'am," I start to say.

"You're in a heap of trouble, Boot," Representative Bridges admits. She sighs and leans on the table for support. "I'll do what I can to help you out."

I nod and look down. Suddenly, my phone starts vibrating again. It's so quiet in the room, we both hear it. "I think that's LaQuota," I say, gesturing to my pocket.

Representative Bridges reaches into my pocket and pulls it out. She shows me the screen.

"It *is* LaQuota!" I say urgently. She's calling, not texting, which surprises me.

Representative Bridges pushes the Answer button and then Speaker.

"LaQuota," I say.

"You good-for-nothin' punk!" LaQuota says, then she launches into a tirade that makes me shrug and Representative Bridges smile. "I trusted you, Boot. I thought you had some sense in that thick skull of yours. First you go by your mom's house—Stang's got one of his war wagons parked out front. They been in here three times, said they'd burn the place down if I didn't turn you over by tomorrow. And then you go and tell them stuffed shirts in Oz about my shop. I got it all on tape, but I'm thinking of deleting it all, along with your skinny butt. Who—"

At that point, Representative Bridges clears her throat loudly enough to cut off LaQuota. The phone goes silent. After a few moments, LaQuota says, "Who's that with you, Boot?"

"My name is Terry Bridges," she says. "I'm the Majority Leader of the House of Representatives."

"I know who you are," LaQuota says. "Boot told me all about you. But how do I know—"

Representative Bridges cuts LaQuota off again. "I am very interested in those tapes you have, LaQuota. And I assure you, I am *not* interested in your, um, line of business."

"You can trust her, LaQuota," I say, looking up at Representative Bridges.

"Yeah, well, that's somethin' coming from a no-good, lying—"

"I think it's fair to say, LaQuota," Representative Bridges interrupts, "that Boot has been dealing with some unusual and extenuating circumstances. You might want to cut him some slack."

I grin at Representative Bridges gratefully.

"Yeah, well, I'll decide that for myself, thank you," LaQuota says.

"Fair enough, LaQuota. Now, how can I get those tapes?"

"I'll meet you," LaQuota says after a brief pause. "And only you. Like I said, I don't trust anyone right now, but your face I'll be able to look up and verify."

"Fine. Name the place and time."

Then LaQuota and Representative Bridges make arrangements to meet within the hour.

Before LaQuota hangs up, she says, "I still have a bone to pick with you, Boot," which makes my heart sink. But then she adds, "But let me tell you something, Representative Bridges, that boy has potential. He could be a real asset to you someday." And that makes my heart sing.

Representative Bridges sets the phone on the table and

looks me squarely in the eye (my other eye is completely swollen shut by now). "I can't do anything to stop the Capitol Police from pressing charges on you, Boot. It's their job. You've violated quite a few laws just being here. But I will do what I can to see that you land on your feet. Deal?"

I nod. "Thank you, ma'am."

"No, Henry—thank you."

Representative Bridges turns and is about to leave, when the door opens. I don't know what I was expecting, but I know that Representative Bridges looks as surprised as me when Senator Charles shuffles in, alone.

"Thank you, Lonnigan," he says to Rhino, who must have escorted him to the door. Then Senator Charles pushes the door closed with his cane.

"Well, well," he says, looking from me to Representative Bridges and back with those icy-blue eyes. "Looks like we have all the rats in one cage."

I can see Representative Bridges bristle. She's been as cool as a cucumber through all of the madness of the evening, but it looks to me like she's going to lose it now. I decide to help her out.

"That's true, now that you're here, Senator *Scrooge*," I say, grinning at him.

A small smile sneaks across Representative Bridges's face.

Senator Charles studies me before responding. "You realize, boy, that all of your actions have merely paved the way for Real Reform and reinforced the urgency for such change. Children like you need to be kept in your place and turned into productive resources, or you will continue to wreak havoc on society. I intend to press my point on this matter before both Houses tomorrow—"

"No, Marcus," Representative Bridges interrupts, matching Senator Charles's frosty tone. "This boy's actions have exposed the cynical, corrupt underbelly of your operation. It is you and your sponsors—" Representative Bridges pauses and turns to me. "What did Lucy like to call them?"

I know what she means right away. "Rich Supremacists."

Representative Bridges nods and faces Senator Charles defiantly. "It is you and your Rich Supremacist friends who continue to wreak havoc on society. Real Reform will be exposed for the fraud that it is...and so will you!" With that, she maneuvers around Senator Charles and tries to leave the room, but Senator Charles grabs her arm.

"On the contrary, Terry," Senator Charles says with a mixture of disdain and delight. "Harboring a fugitive is grounds for expulsion. Your future here in Congress, and your bill, are doomed. I would take a good look around your office before the vote tomorrow. It just may be your last." With that, he lets go of her arm and chuckles sadistically.

Representative Bridges glares at him. She's clearly biting her tongue. After a brief moment, she spins away, opens the door, and leaves.

Senator Charles stands and stares at me for a moment longer, leaning on his cane. He smiles wickedly, like he's got something up his sleeve, then turns and follows Representative Bridges out.

LIFE SENTENCE

I know I kept telling Ms. Verita I had nothing to lose if I got caught, but now that I've been here in juvie for almost a week, awaiting trial, I realize I did have something to lose. Actually, I had lots to lose, but mostly my freedom. It wasn't much freedom, hemmed in as it was by my street life and by being so poor and all—I'd be lying if I didn't admit that I mostly felt trapped—but now I see that it was something.

For the first time in my life, I feel bad for my dad. He's doing a life sentence in a place far worse than this with no chance of parole until he's nearly sixty years old. Don't get me wrong, he deserves to be in jail, if for no other reason than the way he treated my mom—beating and abusing her. But did he deserve to be born into poverty, into a social order whose chance to live the good life is less likely than getting struck by lightning?

I don't have many good memories of my dad. And the

ones I do have I keep locked away; but one comes to me now, unbidden, and catches me by surprise:

My dad always loved trains. He used to tell me the story of how he first arrived in Washington, DC, stowing away on a cargo train that was passing through South Carolina. It was the first time he'd ever been outside Barnwell County.

When I was little, just about the only toy I had that was brand new was a model train my dad brought home for Christmas. I remember sitting in our apartment, running the train around and around on its track. Eventually, it broke.

I don't remember what happened to my toy train after that, but the memory I have now is of a trip we took to New York City when I was five or six years old. It was the only time in my life I'd ever been outside DC. On the way home, we stopped at the Northlandz Train Museum in Flemington, New Jersey. I don't remember much about the trip except the tall skyscrapers, and that we stayed in a motel in New Jersey, but I do remember the museum: miles and miles of miniature trains running through incredible landscapes—mountain passes, prairies, rivers spanned by magnificent bridges and trestles, mining towns, quaint little villages, big cities, and more, much more. I was too little to know this at the time, but it was like a tiny replica of America, our history told in miniature. And trains—trains connected it all.

My dad was mesmerized, and I was, too. To him, a train meant opportunity. We spent hours there while my mom sat outside smoking cigarettes because it was too claustrophobic for her. That was the closest I'd ever been to my dad. It's the best memory I keep of him.

Sitting here by myself, incarcerated, I think I understand my dad better, now. To him, it wasn't just that trains meant opportunity; they meant freedom—a chance to explore the wide world, to see America, to shed the suffocating coils of the ghetto.

In his own warped way, Senator Charles is right. There is a lot more that people like me can contribute to the world. But he's wrong about how to make it happen. A work house is not an opportunity for a kid. It's a life sentence. Even the real Scrooge figured that out.

As I sit here and look at the grid of sunlight on the grimy stone floor of my little room, I hear Ms. Verita's voice telling me that even little changes in Washington, DC, can make a big difference in the world.

I sure hope she's right, because I'm feeling pretty defeated right now. That wily coyote Senator Charles is probably getting off scot-free and I'm sitting here in detention. At least Julien is likely to get what's coming to him. I guess that's something. Although I can't even be sure of that. I've been in a news vacuum since I got here. No one's called or come by. It's like I'm already forgotten, back to being invisible, back to the obscurity I was living in before I escaped Southeast and moved into the Capitol. I thought Ms. Verita would have at least sent some kind of message to me, but maybe she's still in the hospital. I just hope to God she's not dead.

Just then, I hear the guard call my name (well, not really my name, but it's the name I'm used to hearing).

"Kid," he says. "Get your lazy butt off that bed. Visitor here to see you."

Visitor? I know my mom wouldn't (couldn't) make the trip, even though I texted her to tell her where they were taking me before they confiscated my phone. Maybe it's Ms. Verita! I try not to show any emotion or let myself get excited. More likely, it's an investigator or social worker from the courthouse.

The guard escorts me down the hall to the visitation room. It's a bunch of cubbies with thick glass separating the inmates (they call us residents) and their visitors. It's just like you see in the movies, except there's no old-fashioned phone. The place is miked up on either side, so you can just talk.

When I see who the visitor is, I freeze.

"Move it, kid," the guard says gruffly. "You don't have all day."

I shuffle over to the cubby. The look of surprise must still be etched into my face, because Representative Bridges laughs.

"Surprised to see me, Boot?"

I nod. "Yes, ma'am."

"Please call me Terry, Boot. I'm not in the Capitol and there are no spotlights on us."

"Yes, Ms. Terry."

"Just Terry," she says, and her smile is warm and genuine. I'm still surprised as heck.

She stares at me for a while—long enough for me to start fidgeting, but I say nothing. She's the one visiting *me*. What's there for me to say?

"I'll bet you're wondering about Ms. Verita," Terry says at last.

I nod and look up eagerly.

"She'll be fine," Terry assures me. "The bullet only grazed her ribs. But she did suffer a concussion when she hit her head. She's sore, but she's at home now, recuperating."

I'm so relieved I don't know what to say. I look down at my feet.

"She wanted to come by as soon as she was out of the hospital," Terry adds, "but the doctors wouldn't allow it. And we had some things to clear up first."

I nod, but I'm thinking, *what things?*

"You know, Boot," Terry says. Her voice is soft and comforting—like a mother talking to her son. "You're a hero. A national hero."

I look up at her and frown. I may be a naïve teen, but I'm no fool.

She sees my disbelief and smiles. Then she nods to several issues of *The Washington Post* that she's fanned out across the small desk. The headlines are enormous:

"Capitol Kid Exposes Clandestine Plot," "Senator Charles Indicted in Federal Probe," "Democracy First Likely to Pass Congress," and the final one, "A New Era for Education in America!" This one has two subtitles: "Campaign Finance Reform—At Last," and "Congress: Breaking News, Broken."

Representative Bridges lets me take in the headlines. My eyes grow wider as I read each one. She's hiding the last one, which she eases out from under the stack. There's another big banner headline, just like the others, but I'm afraid to read it because I see my name in it. I focus instead on a smaller headline below that reads, "Art Heist Foiled by Attic Ward." But the big headline screams at me. I can't ignore it: "Capitol Kid Exonerated by Congressional Vote, Presidential Pardon Imminent."

My jaw drops. Slowly, my eyes meet Terry's. The look on my face must say, *Is it true?* because she nods.

"That's right, Boot," she whispers. She hesitates before adding, "As soon as I received the call from the President, I rushed over here. It's a shame it took an internal scandal to get Congress to finally do the right thing. But it's happened. Democracy First is now the law of the land. And I have a feeling there will be a lot more constructive legislation coming out of the next Congress." She pauses again. "We have you to thank for getting Washington back on track again."

"Now what?" I say. I didn't really mean to say it; I was just thinking out loud.

"Now?" At first she looks surprised, but she has her answer ready. "Well, Boot, I've come to take you home." The look on Terry's face confuses me. It's like she's trying to hug me with her eyes.

"Home," I say. The word means nothing to me. The best home I ever had—the Capitol Building—is not an option for me and I can't go back to the nabe. Again, Terry must be reading my mind.

"Lucy—I mean, Ms. Verita—and I have reached out to your mom. We're getting her help in a rehab center, but she told us that she's in no shape to take care of you."

Terry stops to let the words sink in. The part about speaking with my mom is a surprise—I immediately wonder if they went to see her and how they got past Stang— but my mom's comment is not. *I've* been the one taking care of *her* since I was eight.

"She's agreed to turn you over to my custody...temporarily." Again she pauses. This time I look up at her. What's Terry saying? But I don't ask; I just stare in disbelief.

Terry laughs. It's warm and genuine. "Ever since my husband died in Afghanistan, I've been living alone on a farm that's too big for me—back in Minnesota. Have you ever been to a farm, Boot? With horses and goats and other animals? We grow corn, too."

I shake my head.

"Well, I'd like to take you there for the Christmas holiday. Lucy has agreed to join us."

Finally, I find some words. My voice cracks. "What are you saying, Ms. Bridges?"

"Terry, please call me Terry." She stares at me, but it's friendly, and there's a gleam in her eye. "I'd like to get to know you a little more, Boot, before you go off to school. And, if it works out, I'd like to offer you an internship in my office."

I stare down at the floor. On the one hand, this is all too good to be true, but I'm also scared. "What do you mean by school?"

Terry smiles. "Lucy and I have made special arrangements with a private boarding school in the District. They've agreed to allow you to attend on a trial basis. That will be your new home."

"But who's gonna pay—"

"They're offering you a scholarship based on your meritorious service." Terry holds up the last newspaper with the headline about the President exonerating me. "But it all depends on your performance, Boot."

For a while I don't say anything—maybe I'm learning

to keep my mouth shut. More likely it's because my head is spinning. Then I accidentally say what's on my mind. "What if I fail?"

"What do you have to lose?" Terry asks.

Now she's talking my language. I start to smile—it spreads across my face like a rash, exposing my chipped tooth. I shrug and tilt my head playfully, then I tell her, "I suppose I could always ditch school and move into the Supreme Court."

I get Terry with that one. She's laughing so hard she can't even speak.

HOME SWEET HOME

*H*orses are deceptive creatures. They look like they should be dangerous, so big and powerful, like they could run you right over, or kick you over a fence, or crush your arm with a single bite. But they don't use their power like that. It's their long lashes and tender eyes that give them away.

I like Terry's mustang; his name's Spot. Maybe it's because I think of the other Stang, back home—I mean in Southeast—and the contrast makes me laugh.

Terry told me that the investigators found evidence on the wire I was wearing that will put Stang away for life. I guess I forgot I had the wire on when I went to visit my mom. Stang screwed himself when he admitted to killing The Wizard, supplying my mom with drugs, and threatening to make an example out of me. Sometimes you get what you got coming.

According to Terry, it took the investigators a while to get LaQuota to turn over the Stang recordings because she was afraid of what his crew would do to her. They had to threaten to shut her down and arrest her for dealing in trafficked goods before she agreed.

I like Spot because he lets me rub his nose and ride him.

Right now, I'm sitting on a fence by myself, watching the sun set over the hills while the horses roam around their field, stamping their feet to keep warm. Never seen anything so beautiful in all my life. Not even the view of the Mall from on top of the Capitol Building at night compares with this. I come out here every evening by myself, even though it's cold, to watch the sun go down. Somehow, it reminds me of that Animal Planet show I watched about the Serengeti. Only, this is a kinder, gentler version. I still want to go see the plains of Africa someday, but I'm content to experience America's other wilderness, too. There's snow on the ground—not much—but here the snow stays white, except for this time of day when it takes on the rosy hue of the sky.

I feel like this is all a dream, like maybe I'm back in the Northlandz Train Museum and I got sucked into one of its idyllic scenes. I keep thinking I'm going to wake up in the hallway of my mom's crack house.

Before we came up here for the holiday, Ms. Verita took me over to the private school to meet some of the teachers and the other kids. They all seemed really nice to me, but I'm afraid I won't fit in. Guess I'll just have to cross that bridge when I get there.

It was Lana who helped us all out. I knew we could count on her, although I was a bit surprised when Representative Bridges—I mean Terry—told me all about it on the ride back from juvie. Turns out Lana was the one who

Julien assigned to work with a guy from IT to set up those surveillance servers in his office. She took pictures of everything, just to cover herself. And she had emails and texts that confirmed Julien had ordered her to set up the surveillance system.

But I was wrong about one thing: When I told Ms. Verita that I saw Julien on a surveillance video handing someone an envelope stuffed with cash, it was the IT guy, not another politician. According to Terry, he was paid more than a hundred thousand dollars to set up the illegal surveillance system, and from what I can tell, he earned his money. That IT guy was no slouch. Not only did he write the trojan, but he also had backup servers wired into Julien's closet that Julien never knew about. So, when Lana finally came forward, she corroborated everything I said about Julien's surveillance scheme. The IT guy even installed his own surveillance camera and microphone inside Julien's office—a watcher watching the watcher. Or, as LaQuota put it, "a blackmailer blackmailing the blackmailers." Like I said, he was no slouch. I'll bet he was from the streets, too. He must have known that it would turn bad at some point, and he wanted to have a Get Out of Jail Free card. The Feds gave him immunity for turning over his surveillance files. Lana got immunity, too. That's how they nabbed Senator Charles. They had him in Julien's office on more than one occasion discussing what they'd learned from tapping all those laptops. Not just laptops—they were tapping tablets and smartphones, too.

Even if Senator Scrooge beats the criminal charges, which Terry thinks is likely, his career is over and he'll be forever in the Hall of Shame. Like I said, sometimes you get what you got coming to you.

I asked Terry if she could get a couple of those black sheen jackets with stitched white letters that say *Member of Congress* for LaQuota and Dottie. Terry made it happen. I haven't heard from Dottie, but that should square us since I ruined her nice thermal hoodie.

Ant-Man texts me nearly every day to see how I'm doing.

Terry says she'd be happy to fly him out for a few days, but I'm not ready to hook up with anyone from Southeast just yet. I want to see my mom first. Christmas is next week. We have plans to see each other right after. I'm looking forward to it, but I'm nervous, too. She'll be sober by then. I'm not sure I'll know what to say to her. Not sure she'll know what to say to me.

Just then, I hear the door to the house slam. I turn to see Ms. Verita coming toward me. She's bundled up like an Eskimo.

"Brrr! It's cold out here," she says, walking up beside me. She rests her arms on the fence. "Wow, that's a beautiful view."

"Sure is."

"But it's too cold for my thin L.A. blood," Ms. Verita complains. "Demasiado frio."

But I can tell she's happy to be out here, watching the sun set.

"Yeah, pero vale la pena," I say. "It's worth it."

We watch the sun as it sinks below the horizon. Neither of us says anything. What's there to say? Words don't do this kind of spectacle justice. As the last ray vanishes from the sky, I start to think about the future.

Ms. Verita says I should go into computer science—she says I'm talented enough to become one of those Silicon Valley billionaires.

"You mean Rich Supremacist?" I joke with her.

"¡No, así no!" she declares. "Not everyone with money is a supremacist, Boot. In fact, some are quite humble, and quite generous. I think that's how you would be."

It's nice of her to say so, to have someone believe in me. I figure if I'm the lucky stiff who got struck by lightning (the good kind) and found a ticket out of the streets, I'd want to pay it back. I'd want to see if I can make lightning strike more often for kids like me. For the Have Nots.

Seeing how beautiful this country is, I feel the desire to pay it back more than ever. I'll probably study computer science so I get good grades.

But I know what I really want to do when I grow up.

I want to make a difference.

I want to be a senator.

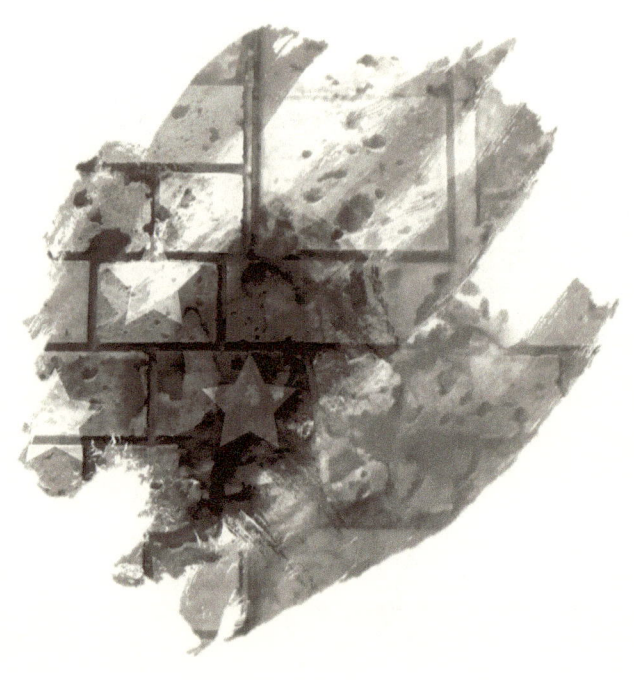

MORE FUN CAPITOL FACTS

The Capitol Building of the United States has a rich and storied past. Here are some more fun facts to complement what Boot shares in his story:

In 1793, Thomas Jefferson held a competition for the design of the Capitol Building, offering the winner $500 (which would be roughly $10,000 today). No entries were selected until an amateur architect, Dr. William Thornton, submitted a design that both Jefferson and Washington fell in love with. Because the competition was closed, it was rumored that he did not win the prize; however, the historical record suggests that he did win the prize money along with a building lot in the city of Washington.

George Washington laid the first cornerstone for the Capitol Building on September 18, 1793. Following the Masonic ceremony, there was a big celebration that day which included the first barbecue and band on the Capitol grounds.

In 1814, British troops set fire to the Capitol, but that was a lucky day because a rainstorm prevented it from burning to the ground.

From its simple roots, the Capitol Building is now part of a complex of more than fifteen major buildings, including six buildings to support the House of Representatives, three buildings for the Senate, three for the Library of Congress, and the Conservatory and Visitor Center.

Since 1909, when it was just a monorail with wicker seats, a subway has run through the Capitol complex carrying politicians and their staff between office buildings and the Capitol.

During the Civil War it really was common for representatives and senators to carry concealed knives and guns with them into the Capitol Building.

In 1858, there was an old-fashioned bar brawl on the floor of the U.S. House of Representatives that started when South Carolina Democrat Laurence Keitt exchanged insults with Pennsylvania Republican Galusha Grow. Soon they were exchanging blows and bedlam erupted on the House floor. The disputed topic—slavery.

A blood stain still remains on the white marble staircase where former congressman Taulbee was shot in 1890 by the reporter Kincaid inside the Capitol Building.

The first African-American to serve a full term in the United States Senate was from (drum roll) Mississippi! Senator Blanche Bruce was born a slave and was elected by the Mississippi state legislature in 1875. (Back then, senators were elected by state Houses). He was a member of the Republican Party.

The first state to elect an African-American to the United States Congress was South Carolina. Congressman Joseph Rainey, a former slave, was elected in 1870 and he, too, was a member of the Republican Party.

It was not until 1917 that the first woman, Jeannette Rankin, served in Congress, and she was elected (1916) four years before the Nineteenth Amendment to the Constitution guaranteed women the right to vote (1920). How was that possible? Because progressives in Montana granted women the right to vote in 1914 and Congressperson Rankin was elected in Montana.

Hattie Caraway of Arkansas was the first woman elected to the United States Senate in 1932. She had already served for a year when she was appointed to serve the remainder of her husband's term after he died in 1931.

The Candy Desk of the United States Senate was first established by California Senator George Murphy in 1965, who must have had a powerful sweet tooth to defy the Senate rules that don't allow eating on the Senate floor.

The salary of a US senator in the 1850s was $3,000 per year, which would be about $85,000 today. In 1925, a US senator earned $7,500 per year, which would be about $100,000 today. But today, US senators earn $174,000. Hmmm?!

References

1. "Candy Desk." U.S. Senate website, Senate History, http://www.senate.gov/artandhistory/art/special/Desks/hdetail.cfm

2. "Traditions of the United States Senate." U.S. Senate website, Senate History, http://www.senate.gov/reference/reference_index_subjects/Traditions_of_the_Senate_vrd.htm.

3. "The Caning of Senator Charles Sumner." U.S. Senate website, Senate History, http://www.senate.gov/artandhistory/history/minute/The_Caning_of_Senator_Charles_Sumner.htm..

4. "The Most Infamous Floor Brawl in the History of the U.S. House of Representatives." U.S. House of Representatives website, House History, http://history.house.gov/Historical-Highlights/1851-1900/The-most-infamous-floor-brawl-in-the-history-of-the-U-S--House-of-Representatives/.

5. "A Historic Killing in the Capitol Building." Morning Edition, National Public Radio, Peter Overby, February 19, 2007.

6. "Senate Fistfight." U.S. Senate website, Senate History, http://www.senate.gov/artandhistory/history/minute/Senate_Fistfight.htm.

7. "Filibuster and Cloture." U.S. Senate website, Senate History, http://www.senate.gov/artandhistory/history/common/briefing/Filibuster_Cloture.htm.

8. Swislocki, Allie. "Secrets of the Capitol Grounds: Olmsted's Summerhouse." U.S. Capitol Historical Society (blog) January 26, 2012 https://uschs.wordpress.com/2012/01/26/secrets-of-the-capitol-grounds-olmsteds-summerhouse/.

9. "My Capitol." U.S. Capitol Visitor Center website, https://www.visitthecapitol.gov/sites/default/files/documents/content/brochure/2503/my-capitol-student-selfguideen.pdf.

10. "Nature at the Capitol – The Statue of Freedom." Architect of the Capitol (blog), September 24, 2013, http://www.aoc.gov/blog/nature-capitol-statue-freedom.

11. "Dr. William Thornton." Architect of the Capitol website, Who We Are, http://www.aoc.gov/architect-of-the-capitol/dr-william-thornton.

TECH TALK

*B*oot is a pretty talented teen who has managed to pick up some amazing technical skills. Here's a non-techie rundown of some of the things he learned:

Smartphone Malware — Boot's description of breaking into Rhino's phone is a simplification of a malware attack, but not by much. Apple iPhones tend to be more secure than Android and Windows phones, but all are vulnerable to determined hackers and cyber attackers. Jailbreaking is the term for opening access to the iOS root directory, which then allows iPhone users (or hackers) to modify their phone's settings and access non-Apple app store apps. It's also a way to quickly acquire unwanted malware. Rooting is the equivalent process for Android phones.

Command Shell and Grep — A command shell is a

native operating system (OS) terminal or console that accepts operating system commands such as grep, which is a Unix (and Linux) command for searching through directories and files. All graphical user interfaces (GUIs) provide some kind of command shell to their native OS, like the one Boot was using to search Ms. Verita's laptop and log in to Julien's server.

Trojan — The category of viruses that tend to be more difficult to detect and more malicious than the average malware virus because, like their namesake Trojan Horse, they are disguised as benevolent files or software that, when they begin to execute, inflict quite a bit of damage to the unsuspecting user, such as enabling webcams, function keys, opening ports, and allowing the kinds of espionage that Julien almost got away with!

HTTP, HTML, and CSS — Acronyms for the protocols and software languages that govern web design. HTTP stands for hypertext transfer protocol. HTML for hypertext markup language, and CSS for cascading style sheet. Of course, there are many other languages and protocols used for web design and development, but Ms. Verita only learned the basics, which was enough to help out her and Boot in a pinch!

VPN — Most companies and government agencies run their own private networks for security purposes. But, to provide broader access to those private networks for, say, telecommuting employees, they set up virtual private networks that allow the use of the

Internet (public networks) to access their private networks. Boot accessed the Congressional VPN by first hacking into Rhino's smartphone.

Tunneling — Since Julien set up his own small private network to house all of his illegal servers, Boot needed a way to get from the Congressional VPN to Julien's private network. Tunneling provides a way to access and transfer data between disjointed networks.

IP Addresses – An Internet protocol address is simply a unique string of numbers that identifies a computer on a network. IP addresses can be thought of as street addresses or phone numbers. They are managed by directories. Boot looked up the IP address of Julien's illegal servers in the IP directory to learn where they were located. Most likely, if Julien were a real hacker, he would not have allowed his IP address to have a physical location associated with it in the directory that Boot was searching. But, hey, this is fiction and Julien isn't that smart anyway!

Ports — A computer port serves as an interface between a computer and other computers or devices. Like a door, an open port is needed to be able to access another computer. Thus, the trojan virus that Boot loaded onto Julien's server opened a port—door—for him to access Julien's server. See PuTTY.

Black Beauty — Believe it or not, these kinds of dastardly black boxes really do exist and can be purchased online if you know the right underground sources. Being a resourceful teen, Boot manages to acquire one, which allows him to break into Julien's server. Beware! Public Wi-Fi networks are very susceptible to these kinds of devices and hackers.

FTP — FTP does not stand for Fiery-Tempered Politician, although… Rather, FTP stands for file transfer protocol, which is one of the most common ways to transfer files between remote computers. When he gets back to his "suite," Boot uses FTP to copy all of the files from Julien's server, which he then promptly loses playing games in the Senate Dining Room.

PuTTY — This is not the Silly or Thinking kind of putty! PuTTY is an open source terminal emulator that provides a command shell (see Command Shell) interface to a remote computer. Although PuTTY appears not to have a definitive meaning for its acronym, TTY stands for teletype, which is what early generation computers used as input (literally typewriter and paper). Boot used this open-source software to access Julien's server.

Crowdsourcing — Enlisting a typically large and random group of people via the Internet to participate in a project, provide a service, or generally collaborate. Although Bing Now is still a hypothetical Microsoft app (at the moment), it's based on a real Microsoft technology that could have worked the way Boot tried to use it to entrap Julien.

Blade Servers — A popular type of computer hardware architecture that allows multiple servers to be slid into (or out of) a single chassis. In the case of Julien's spying operation, it enabled him to quickly expand the capacity of his hardware as he captured more and more files from unsuspecting politicians all across the Capitol.

Linux — An open-source operating system that is similar to Unix. Popular for web servers, but not so much for home computers. True techies like Boot tend to prefer Linux over most other operating systems because of its open-source design and logical operating system constructs.

ACKNOWLEDGMENTS

This tale owes its inspiration to a Maret School field trip to the United States Capitol Building (for my son Sawyer's class) made possible by J.P. Dowd, Chief of Staff for Senator Patrick Leahy.

I also owe a great debt of gratitude to Chelsea Apple (and her colleagues at JKS Communications) whose fabulous editorial insights helped to shape my early efforts into a clear and cogent story.

As always, my wife Brenda's eagle eye and my son Sawyer's boundless enthusiasm make my stories better than anything I could achieve without them.

www.ingramcontent.com/pod-product-compliance
Lightning Source LLC
Chambersburg PA
CBHW021243260626
47155CB00004BA/1287